"Twisting the Needle"

Book Three In the Dr. Ma Mystery Series

By Lenore Maio

Dedication

To my family, friends, patients, and clients who inspire me every day.

To my Tech support guy, Barron Snyder. Thank you.

To my readers. Having the courage and vision to 'see' is simple. Taking the time to 'say' is more complex. Translating my story to a Universal language is well, a work in progress.

Thank you.

Introduction….from Dr. Ma

Things never seem to go according to plan. That is because plans are products of the imagination. They are created to give us the false sense of progress when everything is unfolding according to the Universal Design.

I like to think I am part of the Universal design. My name is Dr. Ma and I am an Elemental Dragon. I have been on the Earthly plane for more than two thousand years, doing my job. My job of protecting humans from Otherworldly beings who would do them harm.

My partner for the last thousand years is my constant companion, David. He is an Elemental Tiger. Together we form the perfect circle of Yin and Yang. I had another partner before David. He is gone now from this Earthly plane of existence.

My human guise this time around is that of an Acupuncture Physician. David is also a Traditional Chinese Medicine doctor. We have a practice in West Palm Beach, Florida. Next door to our Clinic we run a martial arts school. The Mugen Dojo.

As I said, things never go according to plan. I like to go with the flow. As long as it goes my way that is.

My private solicitor Allistair McGowan has been with me since my first manifestation. He makes sure I have all the resources I need lifetime after lifetime to make things go my way here on Earth.

As an Elemental Water Snake, he is a very 'grounded' kind of guy. Don't get me started on where he fits into the *balance* of the Universe!

My human friends, Winnie my Clinic manager and Jeremy Brenner, the Palm Beach Police detective that David and I help solve murders, are important to my plans this time around.

I say Jeremy helps us, but I think in the opinion of his law enforcement colleagues, we help him.

Anyway, we are going to be in South Africa, South Florida, and New York City for this case, so put on your seatbelt and hang tight! Yes, we will take the jets. I can't carry everybody with me when I fly as a dragon!

Prologue - Luohu Tiger Reserve, South Africa

It wasn't hard to get past security when you could afford a bribe that was greater than two months of the guard's salary. The sparse brush of the plains in the Luohu Tiger Reserve, South Africa, wouldn't hide the animals (or people) they were here to poach. Not from the night vision he was given to use for that purpose.

The dark haired, dark skinned man had the bribe for the guard and anything else he needed in the dusty khaki utility vest he wore. His eyes glowed slightly in the dark. Not quite Otherworldly, not the tell-tale lapis blue. Something else, something magically created.

The trucks and automatic weapons were of very good quality. All this made sure he had a willing group of high level criminals to do what *she* wanted of him.

The campsite was brightly lit, a surprise to his men but not to him. He was here for the humans at the camp. The people, not the animals, were his main target. His men just didn't know it. Getting the greedy criminals he had hired to make a quick detour from poaching, to kill some tourists for their money and possessions, was easy.

Telling them that there was a pretty, young, white woman that may make a good sale was the clincher. She was never going to make it to any black market he knew, but it sounded good enough for them. The sound of their truck engines as they approached was loud in the relative silence of the South African plains.

There was confusion among the camp's perimeter guards at first. They wouldn't know they had been betrayed by their own guy for a nice bribe. At first they would probably think someone was coming from the Reserve. They would be thinking that something may have happened.

By the time the shooting began, it would be too late to have any more thoughts. He wasn't planning on any of them surviving.

The only survivor would be himself, and the man who became the Tiger. Not just a tiger, but a massive beast. Steel grey coat, slender black stripes, about a thousand pounds of power was what he had been told.

He knew that his men would kill the camp guards and then probably be killed by the Tiger. In a blur of blood, teeth, and claws. Their machete's and automatic rifles were not good enough to protect them from his vicious response to their attack. No, not nearly enough to fight back against the massive physical power he would display in his Elemental Tiger form.

All he, her minion, had to do to please her and keep living himself, was to shoot the Tiger with the crossbow bolt she gave him. The one she told him not to scratch himself with. The one dipped in poison.

The primal scream the Tiger let loose before jumping into the fight almost unnerved him completely. Hands shaking, he had to re-notch the bolt before letting it fly. Humans would not have heard that blood curdling cry from the massive tiger that was ripping his men to shreds. Otherworldly ears only, of course, would hear him. Like *his* new Otherworldly ears. The ones she had given him with his new form.

He turned to run after letting the bolt fly and saw the ethereal manifestation of the Dragon. She wasn't actually here. Her glittering black skin of fine scales, glowing yellow rimmed eyes and magnificent wingspan weren't tangible. Despite that, the sight chilled him, bringing him to a temporary stop.

"Why was she here?" he thought. The scream and the size of the Tiger were enough, the sight of the Dragon there, even in Spirit form, was the last straw. He threw down the crossbow and ran. He found the dirt bike he had hidden in the brush easily with the night vision, and took off in a plume of dirt.

The noise of his engine would be lost within the sounds of engines and loud voices, still miles away. Voices from more criminals in more trucks. Coming to share in the spoils of the first group, as he had planned.

The scent of oil, gasoline and sweat drifted lightly on the air. He watched the tiger transform back into a man as he rode almost parallel to the campsite to escape. "Magnificent. Both just as powerful in appearance," he thought. He watched the man swing the young white woman on his back and begin to run towards the Reserve's lodge.

Veering away and heading out of the Reserve the way he had come in, Circe's minion smiled.

Run, Tiger, run. All that blood circulating will just help the poison work faster. He would be in such good graces with the Sorceress now.

He had a film of dirt covering his teeth when he arrived back in Town, from grinning the entire way.

Table of Contents

Introduction - from Dr. Ma

Prologue - Luohu Tiger Reserve, South Africa

Chapter One - Brenner and Dr. Ma

Chapter Two - How to Raise a Tiger

Chapter Three - David Goes Shopping

Chapter Four - The Dinner Party

Chapter Five - The Body On The Roof

Chapter Six - Life Lessons

Chapter Seven - Evil Lives In Manhattan

Chapter Eight - The Confession

Chapter Nine - A Family Affair

Chapter Ten - Winnie Quits Her Job

Chapter Eleven - Different Directions

Chapter Twelve - Dr. Ma and the Creator

Chapter Thirteen - Everybody Talks

Chapter Fourteen - How To Kill Your Wife

Chapter Fifteen - Life Goes On

Epilogue

Chapter One - Brenner and Dr. Ma

The Spirit Winds she saw were never convenient. They didn't come and go in a timely manner. Their strength, length, and content, were not predictable. But it was the job.

She willingly signed up for this job every next time around. She didn't have to re-manifest. At least she *thought* there was some free will in play there. Two thousand years and she wasn't bored. She willingly came back to protect humans on the Earthly plane from Otherworldly evil doers.

David, her constant companion of one thousand of those years, always came back with her. He was her balance. His Yang to her Yin energy. His powerful Elemental Tiger to her even more powerful Elemental Dragon.

They were a perfect team. Just like her first tiger had been. Her mate that was no longer on this plane of existence. David had been formed to take his place with her. To restore balance. Not to be her mate. Dragons mate for life.

That was no comfort to David. He could only have one *true* mate on this plane. An Elemental Dragon. Come to think of it, David not being able to be her mate was no comfort to her lately either. A thousand years was a long time to be without true intimacy. Oh, they were about as intimate as two beings could be after spending a thousand years together. Just not *that* kind of intimate.

Riding with the Monday night cycling group that left from the base of the Lake Worth bridge was a guilty pleasure for Dr. Ma. They started when Daylight Savings Time ensured they would have a couple hours of waning daylight to burn. The group ride ended for the year, when the South Florida Winter, which was more about shorter days than colder weather, made it a full on, dark ride.

Not that they didn't have headlights and taillights for their bikes during the Winter season. It was more about the elderly snow birds who would run you off the road in the Winter season and leave you lying there. This time of year was definitely safer. If not as exciting.

So, during late Spring, Summer, and early Fall, she left David to handle Tuesday classes at the Dojo and rode with the small group of fast, some elite cyclists, that practically flew along.

One tightly behind the other, they rode east over the bridge and then north on A1A.

The fact that this particular Spirit Wind chose to catch her on her bike just after the ride wasn't endearing its story to Dr. Ma. She would have to pull over and let it come. She was heading into downtown West Palm Beach with night falling. Not the best place to stop all alone either.

Dr. Ma was not afraid of anything on the current Earthly plane. But, she had healthy respect for some things. Things like criminals with guns. If she saw them first, there was no contest. She won. Gunshots could kill her human body. Unlikely with her speed and power, but possible.

Dealing with a Spirit Wind could make her a bit vulnerable. Slower to respond. David would come to her and help her. In Spirit form only. She also couldn't just walk into a crowded restaurant or coffee shop. The slight fugue state she would enter could be enough to have them call an ambulance or law enforcement to help her.

"A little help?" she sent out mentally towards the Intracoastal Waterway, hoping for a response from the Water Sprites that lived there. At least they would be some amount of protection with their limited magic.

She slowed her bike coming west over the Okeechobee Bridge and turned north on Flagler Drive. Pulling off the road and stepping onto the broad concrete walkway that bordered the Intracoastal Waterway, she guided her bike next to her. She saw one of the public benches that dotted the walkway and made her way towards it.

"Dr. Ma?" she heard her name called. Turning her head, she saw her friend, Detective Jeremy Brenner, waving at her out of his car window. "Oh no," she groaned inwardly, "this just gets better and better." She could hear the howling of the Wind, closer now. The last thing she wanted, was to have Jeremy there when it arrived.

Brenner quickly parked his POV (personal off-duty vehicle) in one of the parallel spaces next to the walkway and hopped out. He had been wanting to speak with Ma about a case that NYPD had asked him to consult on yesterday. He followed her to the bench where she leant her bike along the waist high concrete abutment to the Intracoastal Waterway.

Even in the darkening conditions, she could make out Jeremy Brenner's signature good looks. Mixed Irish, English and Scottish family genes produced sandy ginger hair and light blue eyes.

He wore his hair close cropped on a nicely shaped head. Freckles and an easy smile balanced well with his hard physique from various martial arts disciplines. He was a formidable opponent to bad guys at six foot tall, one hundred and eighty pounds.

Ma could feel the Wind now, she could smell the first batch of scents related to the crime. She had no choice but to involve Jeremy. "Please sit down on the bench with me," she said firmly, hurrying to sit down on the bench.

Jeremy Brenner stopped mid sentence and looked at her. He had just started to tell her about his case referral. "Are you alright?" were his first words. The cop was all business in moments when a difficult situation presented itself. He knew immediately that things weren't right.

"Please just go with what is about to happen Jeremy," Ma said, in anything but a pleading tone of voice. She was his martial arts teacher as well as his physician. She was used to giving him direction. "I need you to sit with me and not say or do anything until I am ready. Don't let anything interrupt me. I won't be fully able to respond to any interruption or threat in a few minutes. I will explain later."

Brenner didn't waste time with small talk. Whatever was about to happen didn't matter as much as handling it well. He almost pulled her down onto the bench with him. Anyone passing might have though they were lovers, about to cuddle in the dark. Ma turned to face him and wrapped her arms around his waist to steady herself. She rested her head on his shoulder in the crook of his neck. Then, she went very still.

Jeremy could smell her hair. Her nearness and the intimacy of her embrace was creeping through his tough professional exterior. Dr. Ma was a beautiful woman. He had admired her for years, but she was his martial arts teacher and about twenty years his senior.

Long, impossibly straight hair was pulled into a braid down her back. Inky black, it was set off by her South Florida tan and brilliant lapis blue eyes. Her body was lean and muscled from a lifetime of physical training.

Locked in a gentle, almost loving embrace, his throat felt tight and he fought any response his body may consider to her proximity. She sighed softly into his neck and he bit his lip to stay focused.

Dr. Ma may have seemed quiet and peaceful on the outside, but the raging storm within was causing her a problem. She had called out to David when she first stopped her bike.

Still at the dojo, several students around, David tried to make some quick excuses and escape into the attached Traditional Chinese Medical Clinic. Sosam Li, one of their student teachers, dogged David's steps.

At six foot five inches tall, David's perfectly muscled, lean body, and past shoulder length sun streaked blond hair often kept many students dogging his steps after class. He was usually the last to leave, answering question after question with infinite patience.

Entering the back door of the clinic, it was almost too late. David, hearing the screaming Wind, saw Ma in his mind, resting in Jeremy Brenner's arms on a bench by the Intracoastal Waterway. He pushed his surprised reaction at her circumstances away to try and focus on containing the Wind for her.

She was in the middle of the maelstrom, being buffeted by the strangely strong Wind. She was calling his name. David felt himself pulled into the Spirit vision with her and dropped suddenly to his knees in the hallway. Sosam Li, still right behind him, ran the few steps between them and knelt beside his beloved instructor.

"Sifu!" he shouted, wrapping his arm around David's waist and trying to lift him up. The powerful man felt like he weighed a thousand pounds. "What the hell?" Li thought to himself. A head shorter than his teacher, with a rock hard body from years practicing the martial arts. Li was usually strong enough to manipulate a much greater weight than his own.

David knew he had to grapple the Wind for Ma, or risk both of them being lost in the melee until it was over. Lost and perhaps missing important information about a murder they could not recover when it was gone.

He gave a last, superhuman effort to press the energy of the Wind between his powerful hands. Li watched a brighter patch of light than the surrounding hallway bloom between David's hands.

Sosam Li had seen great masters manipulate Qi. From training with David and Dr. Ma for many years, he knew they were both the greatest of all masters he had ever seen.

David's lapis blue eyes were closed while he knelt in the hallway, pressing the ball of Qi between his hands. Rolling the ball North and South, he was compressing the images whirling around Dr. Ma in the vision. Holding them still.

On her end, Ma was finally starting to make sense of the images and sensations tearing at her in a cyclone of activity. She could see David kneeling in the hallway of their Clinic. Sosam Li was next to him, watching the ball of Qi in David's hands. "Oh no," Ma thought briefly, "that will have to be dealt with."

Immersing herself in the Spirit Wind, Ma let every detail available of the crime absorb into her very essence. All she had to do was be a sponge and the information would attach itself. Her inner vision was fully open. Safe in Jeremy's arms she could let go and allow it to saturate her being.

This one was powerful. She could see David trembling slightly with the effort to contain it. The only Wind that powerful would be influenced by an Adept of some sort. Ma knew the identity of the Spirit would be revealed fully when they were done. She had absorbed enough. She nodded slightly to David.

Jeremy felt her stir slightly in his arms. It had been at least five minutes since Ma had embraced him and gone still. He couldn't see his watch in the dark. His arms were wrapped around her to make them look more natural sitting together. His eyes watched the darkness like any good cop. Watching for any threat to come their way.

At the Clinic, David spun the ball of Qi to an East and West position and let it free. Sosam Li watched the glow fade from between David's hands as he slumped forward, groaning. "I was NOT expecting THAT," David mumbled. It had been very strong, that Wind. Containing them when they first arrived was not as difficult as wrestling them into submission when they were in full rampage mode. He vaguely wondered, "Who died? Surely a powerful Adept."

Remembering suddenly that Li was kneeling next to him, holding him up, David stood unsteadily and pulled his student up with him. They ended up standing very close in the hallway. Li closed the distance and put his arms around him, as if still holding him up. "Sifu, what happened?" Li asked.

David saw the barely concealed emotion in his student's deep brown eyes. The gleaming black hair Li sported was still covered by a bandana in typical martial arts training style. His training attire of black stretch pants and a coolmax t-shirt with the school's logo, was dry compared to David's. Sosam never sweated much.

Sensing the deep attraction Li felt for him, he gently put his hands on his student's arms, pulling back out of his semi embrace. Li's face fell suddenly. "Sosam," David said softly, almost face to face with the younger man. "I'm fine, thank you so much for helping me."

Li looked up, quickly hiding his disappointment that David had pulled away. Li had been gay all his life, and both his instructors knew about him. It didn't matter to them in the least.

Except for his attraction to David. The Mugen Dojo had an iron clad 'no fraternization' between students and teachers code. Period. As it should be.

Li understood, but had never given up hope. He knew many gay men in Palm Beach who were interested in David. While it seemed the sexy martial arts teacher and acupuncture physician was open and friendly with everyone who flirted with him, he didn't have a girlfriend or boyfriend. Li thought it was just odd. Hot guy, no action. Odd.

"I think my blood sugar was low," David said in explanation. Li was skeptical at best. "I was going to grab some snacks here but, what about me treating you to a late dinner for helping me?" he asked Li.

Sosam Li thought his birthday had just come early. He may never get his instructor into bed in this lifetime, but a couple of hours talking and eating together was more than he usually managed with the shy, gorgeous man.

David watched Li's expression brighten. He grabbed a couple of his raw nut bars from the refrigerator in his office and handed Li one. "Let me take a quick shower," he said to Li. "How about you?" he offered. Li's heart skipped a whole beat. "We have two in the back."

His heart rate returning to normal, Li declined. He wasn't sure taking his clothes off around David was a wise decision on his part. And, he didn't have a change of clothes.

Meanwhile, by the darkened waterfront, Dr. Ma had recovered herself and disentangled from her embrace with Jeremy.

The navy blue, velvety evening had deepened in darkness around them. Less than savory characters were appearing here and there.

"Let's put your bike in my POV and grab some coffee,"Jeremy said to Ma, trying to shake off the intimacy of their recent embrace. "Are you alright? Do I have to take you to a walk-in clinic first or something?"

"No," she said. "I see things Jeremy, that is how I help you with your cases. Sometimes I get a vision and it incapacitates me for a few minutes."

"Oh," Brenner said, nonplussed. What she said was a surprise but it sounded completely truthful, and even plausible. He had seen things like that on TV. He just didn't know he would participate in such an event with Dr. Ma. "So, coffee still sounds good?"

"Great!" Ma said. The particular road bike she was riding tonight broke down easily, and would slip into Jeremy's trunk without an issue. "Why did you flag me down?" she asked.

"I have a case I wanted to consult with you about. From," he began before she interrupted him.

"NYPD?" she asked.

Brenner's mouth hung open. "How in the hell does she do that," he thought. Aloud he just stammered, "Yes."

"I think I may know who your victim is," Ma answered.

Jeremy opened his mouth as if to speak, but their conversation was interrupted by the sudden appearance of a Water Sprite. The creature stood on the concrete barrier wall next to the walkway.

The wall ran the length of the Intracoastal Waterway through West Palm Beach and Lake Worth. It changed in height and decoration as it changed the neighborhoods it protected from rising water.

"Ma-sama," the little creature said in its tinny, metal on metal voice.

"What the f-ck?" Jeremy Brenner said, looking at the little creature.

Too late, Dr. Ma realized he was seeing what she was seeing. Too late, the Water Sprite realized the human detective could see him as clearly as Dr. Ma. Ma looked down and saw Jeremy's hand on her arm. He was probably going to take her bike from her to put in his trunk.

"Was it the contact with her that was helping him see the Otherworldly creature?" she thought.

Brenner was fast. He slipped his arm around Dr. Ma, pulling her behind him in a protective manner. As one arm pulled her back, the other pulled his firearm from its shoulder holster. "Nicely done," Ma couldn't help thinking.

The Sprite froze, too frightened to move.

Dr. Ma moved. She took a step forward with her right foot from behind Brenner, placing her hip in front of his, and shot her right hand across his body by reaching under his outstretched arm. Then, she wrapped her hand around the slide of the automatic weapon.

Too fast to register, she stripped the firearm from his hand. The Water Sprite disappeared with a soft splash and Brenner looked at her in disbelief. "What?" was all he got out.

Dr. Ma went with it. "Have you been drinking? she asked Jeremy in rebuke. "What on earth are you doing?" She had stepped sideways after relieving him of his gun. She still held her bike in one hand and his Glock .45 caliber semi automatic hand gun in the other.

Brenner reached for the firearm, only to have one of Dr. Ma's feet crack into his wrist in a precise strike. His hand went numb. He was recovering from his surprise enough to realize this was a no win situation. Her skills were beyond him and he was still trying to process why he had drawn his gun in the first place.

He was staring hard at the place he had seen the odd looking creature. It was like something out of a movie. Maybe two feet tall at tops, it glowed a soft green with silvery eyes and the general appearance of one of those Troll Dolls from the 60's. His mother had one in her bedroom from her childhood.

He blinked hard and shook his head. Then he walked closer to the retaining wall and looked over it for a moment. It had spoken, the Troll Doll looking creature. Some weird sounding language like rubbing two tin cans together. Looking back at her, he stammered, "Didn't you see it?"

"See what?" Dr. Ma said, her voice neutral. She felt terrible doing this to him. She just didn't know what else to say. Her mind was racing. Jeremy had never seen anything Otherworldly before in her or David's presence. "Did him holding her during the arrival of the Spirit Wind change something?" she thought.

"I must be working too many hours," he said, rubbing his hands over his face. He looked up and held his hand out authoritatively. "Please return my firearm, I am not a danger to anyone, I swear."

She frowned at him and walked closer, looking at him carefully. Handing him his firearm, grip first, muzzle pointing down, and said, "I have never seen you do anything like that. You need to get some sleep or maybe see a doctor."

"Yes. You're my doctor," he said vaguely. "Seriously, you saw nothing?"

"No," she said firmly. Changing the subject and hoping to return things to a semblance of normalcy, she said, "I do have to thank you again for being here for me."

He helped her put her bike, and its now separate front wheel, into his trunk. Closing it, she walked around to the front passenger seat. Jeremy had already opened the door for her. Slipping into the seat she said, "Starbucks?"

Jeremy shook his head affirmatively and got in the drivers side. Starting the engine, he looked over at her and asked, "I suppose you plan on telling me more about what happened back there with you on the bench? Like what you saw and how often this kind of thing happens?"

"Absolutely not Jeremy," Ma answered laughing. "Since when do I tell you everything?"

"Never," he responded quickly. He smiled at her. "I am just glad to have been there when you needed me. If you ever decide to tell me, fine. If not, no worries. I really apologize for freaking out on you and drawing my gun at some imaginary thing. Our secret?"

Ma smiled at Jeremy with real affection. She had become attached to him from working their cases together. Still, there were many things Jeremy would never know about her and David. Much he could never understand.

"I am glad you were there too. Nothing to worry about as far as me telling anyone that you are officially seeing things. You can describe your new imaginary friend to me. Coffee?"

Dr. Ma and David were Traditional Chinese Medical doctors, specializing in Sports Medicine. They had a large Clinic with an attached martial arts school in coastal West Palm Beach, Florida.

Now, in their Traditional Chinese Medicine Clinic, David toweled off after his shower. He was glad that Li had turned down his prior offer to use the second stall and was currently sitting in the beautiful waiting area. Golds and reds were the predominant colors in that room, along with every conceivable shade of green. The overall effect was calming, but also warm and inviting..

"What was I thinking?" he chided himself. He knew Li was gay and very attracted to him. "A shower? In the Clinic, alone with me?" David amazed himself at times. Dressing in a pair of faded jeans and a polo shirt, David joined Sosam Li in the Clinic's waiting area.

"Ready? Thai Express in Lantana, my treat?" he said. He knew it was one of Li's favorite places.

Sosam Li looked at his teacher standing there in his soft, faded jeans and shirt. "He is so incredibly handsome," Li thought. Tousled blond hair pulled back in a loose pony tail, only towel dry. Gorgeous eyes and sharp angles to his face set off a sensuous mouth. His tall frame was an anatomical study of muscle covered in golden tanned skin.

Li sighed. "At least I can show off being with him," he thought. Thai Express had a large gay male clientele. David was a very attentive 'date' when he treated you to dinner. He seemed to hang on your every word when he was with you. Always the perfect, sexy, gentleman. "They will all be so jealous," he thought.

"Let's do it," Li said, hoping it sounded neutral enough. He waved his keys. "I suppose I am driving?"

Everyone knew David didn't drive.

Not everybody knew that it was partly because he was color blind. Every tiger, Elemental or not, was pretty color blind. At least enough to not pass a driving test. David never seemed to have a lack of rides if needed. Li knew he ran most places or walked.

The two of them left out the back door, carefully locking up and activating the alarm. Then they locked up and set the alarm in the dojo next door.

Getting into Li's car, David figured he would see Dr. Ma some time tomorrow. It was their day off. She had a meeting with Allistair, their solicitor, in the morning. They had a lot to discuss after her Spirit Wind vision tonight. Another murder, surely.

Chapter Two - How to Raise a Tiger

Dr. Ma suddenly looked at Allistair. "I know why David has never been as strong as Avo," she said slowly. He watched a silent movie of expressions pass over her features before she spoke again. "And, I know how to make him stronger."

The two of them were sitting in Allistair's private office. Rich furnishings and gleaming wood paneling were set off by chair and desk level lighting. The level of sound proofing rivaled the White House's situation room. You didn't want a typical conversation the attorney heard from his Otherworldly clients getting out. That could be problematic.

Allistair frowned slightly, unsure of what she was saying. The beautiful woman sitting across from him did not often appear uncomfortable with the spoken word. Then her thoughts reached his mind. All the Elementals and many Otherworldly beings could hear each other's thoughts clearly.

"Ohhh," he said grinning. "Now *that* is interesting."

"No it's not," Ma said frowning. She uncharacteristically reached up to smooth back a lock of her long straight hair over the shoulder it had escaped from. I definitely do *NOT* want to go there with him. I am just getting the impression that I will have no choice."

Elegantly attired in a dove gray Lafayette 148 pants suit and her signature Louboutin heels, she appeared flawless. Ageless skin and only the lightest dusting of makeup was paired with a bold, modern piece of jewelry. A large Birkin handbag sat next to her chair on the floor.

"I could try for you," Allistair offered, wiggling his eyebrows. "I wonder what skills I could impart to that handsome beast?" He watched her carefully for her reaction. He was enjoying seeing her discomfort. It hadn't happened very frequently in the more than two millennia they had known each other.

"Stop it," she rebuked him. "You know that the Dragon and the Tiger energies merging are what I am talking about."

"Hey," Allistair said. "If you aren't going to help him out, I might as well do the best I can. Just think of the implications if it worked. We would be the resident Otherworldly power couple on the Earthly plane."

Dr. Ma knew he was kidding, sort of. "You are not to bring up this topic with him," she said firmly, her voice slightly changing in timbre. That meant that her dragon self was closer to the surface than her human guise. "You know his personality. He would do it just to make you happy."

"It could make him happy too," Allistair threw in one final tease. Dr. Ma glowered at him, sitting up straighter in her chair. "Okay fine, but if you fail and he still needs some power boost, I'm his man," he said.

The attorney went back to studying the information spread out before him.

Dr. Ma just looked at him and shook her head. She would find a way around her sudden self revelation, *and* help David retain abilities he gained in each re-manifestation. Without becoming his actual mate.

She was a thousand years older than him in reality, and almost two decades in human years this re-manifestation. Besides, she had one soulmate already.

She just had to figure out the particulars of what made the energy balance stronger when she and Avo had mated. Avo had been her original mate. Another Tiger, sent to her after her first manifestation on Earth. She had spent her first thousand years with him as her companion.

David had been her second Tiger when Avo left. He re-manifested each lifetime by human birth, versus her place marker method. When they got back together, he gained knowledge and power from every lesson she taught him.

Then he lost much of it again when he died. That had been the cycle through their thousand years together. It was very inefficient compared to his predecessor.

She knew she was right in her assumption that their merging of energy would result in a dramatic change in the tiger's abilities. She could accomplish this by taking him as her mate but she simply didn't want to love and lose again. The first time was enough.

"Besides," she thought. "I am a Dragon and Dragons mated for life." Even if it was a Tiger who was her first mate. That made things a little different for her.

The ancient, Chinese mythological power balance between the Dragon and the Tiger representing, Yin and Yang, was what they had been created to replicate. Her first mate, Avo, a Tiger, was her perfect balance. They had been fierce in battle. Then, after a thousand years together, Avo had passed from the Earthly plane.

"You are interrupting my perusal of your new project with the thoughts racing around in your head," Allistair said, looking up at her. "David was sent to you as Avo's replacement."

She and Allistair had been together since the beginning, even before Avo arrived. Allistair had ancient origins like her, long forgotten. He was a powerful Elemental. His transformation was into a massive green Anaconda when he left his human guise.

Snakes represented the Element Water.

"You don't have to listen in," Dr. Ma chided him. "I am just trying to put the pieces together on David's, ah, development."

Allistair nodded absently, already back to his reading. The attorney was somewhat obsessive compulsive regarding contractual details. Exactly what you wanted an attorney to be, of course.

Both Ma and Allistair had wondered how the young tiger, David, never seemed to become the great warrior Ma's first mate had been. Now, she might have the answer. All it would take was for her to have sex with him. Or so she thought. Mating physically or energetically, but not emotionally.

Not that David was weak. Far from it. He had fought with her bravely and viciously through the millennia. "If anything," Ma thought, "he had a greater heart and spirit than Avo." He would have had to, given that he wasn't as powerful in certain ways. He did not seem to have any, what some Otherworldly beings would call, *magical* abilities.

Elementals weren't really considered magical, per se. They could manipulate their element and other elements as they were related to them. Dr. Ma was made from the element Air. Because of this, she could manipulate fire and ice within her body by using the available chemistry in the atmosphere.

David was created from the Element Earth. This is why he had to work so much harder at everything. Air, Fire and Water acted more on Earth than Earth did on them. The biggest thing about the Earth Element was its consistency and vast power. An earthquake could scar the Earth, but not destroy it. It may take many years to heal the destruction, but it would heal.

Allistair, in his Elemental snake form could tell you the history of anything he digested. The two of them also created and maintained an alternative location for the actual Library of Alexandria. The Water and Air Elementals could pass between planes of existence easily. Ma could visit the most. David could not visit any without assistance.

Dr. Ma or Allistair had to take him with them into the Library as needed.

Traveling through planes of existence, transforming into massive and powerful beasts from their daily human guise and displaying feats of human endurance and strength that pulled from their Elemental sources were commonplace. Sometimes that could seem magical, but it was not.

Pulling her musings back to her ever present Tiger companion, she noted another difference between her current Tiger and her first mate. "David never seemed to fear death in his human guise," she thought. She had wondered at times if it was simply a relief from the weight of the life he re-manifested into each time.

Unlike Avo, David's beginnings were painful, torturous. Part of his contract, if that is what you call something like that, was to be reborn in the same circumstances. He also died traumatically, each and every time.

Usually with her holding him.

This was another part of her decision. She already cared about him too much. When he would lie there bleeding out, suffering, and telling her he loved her before he died. It tore her apart from the inside. He was usually dying from saving her life in battle.

"Hey now," Allistair interrupted her thoughts. "No clouding up the peaceful and happy atmosphere I have worked so hard to build here." He waved his hand expansively around the room.

"Stop listening to my thoughts," she said again. "I have accused him of risking his life at times. He seems to run towards death with abandon. Avo never wanted to die. He was more cunning in a fight."

"Avo had you," Allistair commented dryly. "David does not. That is the difference. Something powerful to live for. You know he loves you completely."

She knew he did.

Her cell phone rang, stopping her next comment on the topic of the tiger's strength and power. Allistair went quiet again, studying the paperwork on the new business dealing that Dr. Ma had brought to him. She looked down at the caller ID and answered it. "Yes Jeremy?"

Listening carefully, Ma nodded a few times as Detective Brenner gave her the details of a murder victim found this morning in Palm Beach. A victim related to the case in New York City they were just discussing the night before.

Dr. Ma noticed Allistair looking up at her over his reading glasses. He could hear her thoughts clearly, but not the conversation on the other end of the phone.

"I have to pick up David later tonight from a dinner," Ma said. "It will be late if I know Barry and his faux Hampton clam bake parties, but I want him to be in on the case information from the beginning. Do you want to meet us then or tomorrow?"

Detective Brenner agreed on an early morning breakfast meeting at the Mugen Dojo tomorrow morning. He said he would take their early Tai Chi class. Dr. Ma smiled to herself at this. Jeremy hated morning classes. What he did not seem to dislike was the particular young woman who stood next to him at the front of the class.

Gracie was an Olympic hopeful and a fiery personality, who more than held her own with the intense detective.

"Okay Jeremy," she said. "I will see you in the morning at class. Winnie will have your usual for breakfast afterwards." She hung up the phone, still smiling.

"Since when does Detective Brenner go to morning classes? I thought he was allergic to sunlight?" Allistair asked.

He was referring to the detective's fair, freckled skin. His predominantly Irish heritage blessed him with the ability to acquire a sunburn in a short period of time. "Why do you have that shit eating grin on your face?" the attorney added.

"Watch your language old snake," Ma rebuked him. "Our detective is interested in a certain female student in the morning Tai Chi class I believe. We also have a new murder to help Detective Brenner solve in Palm Beach. Apparently a recently missing young socialite was located sprawled on top of a beach house roof on the island."

Remaining quiet and still, in that very snake like thing he did, Allistair absorbed her information. Sometimes he forgot to blink when he was that still. Good thing most all his clients were Otherworldly and it didn't freak them out a bit.

"She was recently missing from Manhattan," Dr. Ma continued. "The body was only noticed when it started to bloat in the hot sun. Apparently, whoever was driving by thought she was just improving her tan on the hot, clay, barrel tile roof before that."

Dr. Ma was busy typing in a text while she related the chain of events from Detective

Brenner. David was with Barry all day doing their annual 'clean the closet for charity' regimen. He should be reading her text and shaking his head.

David was always amazed at the way humans were killed and disposed of by other humans. She looked up to gauge the attorney's reaction.

Allistair raised his eyebrows inquiringly but didn't comment. His steel gray pinstriped three piece suit was immaculate. The stunning view of the West Palm Beach skyline behind him through floor to ceiling glass widows was remarkable. Tinted shades to see out but not in covered the glass, allowing the beauty and sunlight to filter in. It was just enough to keep the office professional and comfortable.

The attorney had moved his main office closer to Dr. Ma and David in West Palm Beach, at Ma's insistence. The fact that he had fallen madly in love with a rambling modern mansion on Palm Beach island sealed the deal. His Miami mansion had been sold and packed up in no time.

Once the fussy man had immersed himself in the local elegant lifestyle of the island, he never looked back. Miami had become too hectic and overcrowded for him anyway.

The three Elementals had just returned a few days ago from another trip to South Africa. They had to go back and clean up a little detail from their last murder case. The Otherworldly bad guy, or girl in this case, had left a free roaming minion.

The unknown minion had been the one to shoot David with a crossbow while he was there protecting the daughter of a friend. She was visiting a tiger reserve that benefitted from her charitable foundation. How David's whereabouts had been known so *precisely* was still a mystery.

Dr. Ma healed David's near fatal injury in the United States, but they had to go back and kill the leftover minion. It simply wasn't prudent to leave newly Otherworldly beings wandering about to destroy and murder. They had killed Circe, its maker, but the minion needed to be erased as well.

They had begun tracking him from the Luohu Tiger Reserve near Philippolis in the Free State and near Vanderkloof Dam in the Northern Cape of South Africa. He had headed for the

Dam. The Vanderkloof Dam is the second biggest dam in South Africa. Dr. Ma and Allistair were interested in seeing it for themselves.

Apparently the minion was a water sports enthusiast. That, or the Sorceress had arranged to meet him there for some sailing, skiing, and windsurfing.

He was registered at the Vanderkloof Holiday Resort, in a chalet next to the dam. The pay to kill the tiger must have been pretty good. The resort was costly for locals.

They found him further south in the Doornkloof Nature Reserve.

Particularly scenic, it boasted an amazingly mountainous landscape and a collection of deep, shady kloofs grown over with olive, buffalo-thorn and sweet thorn trees.

Mountain reedbuck, buffalo, eland, kudu, the lurking brown hyena, the bat-eared fox and even the odd hedgehog and some 173 bird species including 19 raptors were of much more interest to the tiger than the amazing dam construction.

Dr. Ma had to insist David not transition to his tiger form and check the place out late at night. "I promise I will bring you back here on vacation when we are done," she said.

Allistair looked at her expectantly. "Oh for goodness sake! B*oys!*" she laughed. "You can come too Allistair."

They caught up with Circe's minion at the hiking hut. It was situated on the trail that ran for 2-3 days into the veld. Evidence of recent human activity at the picnic and braai areas on the Seekoei River bank at Roodewal made them cautious, but they saw nobody else in the immediate vicinity.

The young man had had their color eyes. Almost. Not as deeply blue. No yellow ring of a predator. He also had the Sorceress' distinct signature energy. But he wasn't particularly strong. Not yet, and never to be with her gone from the Earthly plane.

David killed him quickly after transforming into his Elemental tiger self. Mauling by a tiger was much more explainable than the way Dr. Ma or Allistair would have killed him. Of course the Elemental snake wouldn't have left a trace of evidence. He just said he wasn't all that hungry right then.

By the time they had returned home, nobody even missed them. Just like nobody was ever going to miss Circe's final minion.

"Thinking about South Africa?" Allistair prompted. He knew the direction of her thoughts, if not always all the particulars.

"Yes," Dr. Ma sighed and got up. "We are still missing the piece of the puzzle that led Circe directly to David and Karen in South Africa. You know that I don't like anything to come back and…" He interrupted her before she could finish.

"Bite you in the butt," the attorney said. "I know, but we turned over every rock we found. It will come out eventually.

Dr. Ma looked around before heading to the large carved wood doors leading into the main office area of McGowan and McGowan. "You have done a very nice job with this place Allistair," she commented.

"Thank you," the fussy man preened for a moment. He stopped to touch a priceless sculpture sitting on a pedestal near the doorway. "I am *quite* happy here," he said.

Dr. Ma grinned back. She and David knew that Allistair had recently met a charming young man that hung on his every word and was happily at his beck and call. No longer needing to pretend, the old plan he had of taking a wife and producing an heir by artificial insemination was retired. He seemed genuinely happy with a male companion.

"So, things are going well with Scott?" she asked. She knew they would just get married and adopt or use Scott as a surrogate for Allistair's next place marker child. Scott would never know what the snake really was, but he would live a luxurious life from then out if the two of them hit it off.

"He is quite charming," Allistair beamed.

"Good for you," Ma said. "Yet you still talk trash about David?" She was smiling broadly now, teasing him.

"Oh my dear," Allistair said, fixing her with a serious stare. "Scott has nothing to do with anything I could ever put together with the

Tiger. Some things you just have to forgive your, ah, partner."

Dr. Ma laughed. "You are comfortably the same my friend," she said to him. "I hope you never change, even for another thousand years."

Allistair opened the door for her and bent to whisper in her ear. "I still have my eye on you too beautiful dragon," he said. "Like David, I am more an opportunist!"

"Get back to work you old lech," she laughed softly. "I will see you soon."

Chapter Three - David Goes Shopping

The knock on his apartment door was brisk and efficient. David had just come out of the shower after a long run. It was his morning off. He opened the door with just a bath towel wrapped around his waist. He was still damp from sweating during his run, despite having toweled off. A second towel was wrapped around his shoulders.

Barry Lorel, David's friend and long time personal stylist stood there smiling. The man was always well groomed, perfectly pressed and meticulously presented. In his early 60's, Barry looked great. A head of silver hair and light blue eyes, paired well with a pink Ralph Loren polo shirt, madras walking shorts and Manolo Blank loafers. A Hermes belt of the same leather hue as the shoes finished the outfit.

Barry raised his eyebrows and lifted his fashionable black framed glasses as he looked David up and down. "My dear man," he said. "Are you trying to tempt me this early, or are all the years I have tried to teach you to dress properly going to waste?"

David laughed and let him in to the impeccably designed, but simple space. Long, floor length windows in the century old stone walls were covered with what seemed like every blooming Vanda orchid of every color. The highly polished wood floor gleamed. Very expensive, but few, pieces of furniture were placed strategically, giving the impression of wealth and taste.

Barry's taste and David's wealth really. "I see the apartment is still as I left it last," Barry sniffed, indicating he hadn't been invited to visit since their last annual wardrobe clean out.

David took the towel off his shoulders and flicked it gently at Barry's butt. "Locker room tactics?" Barry smiled. "Young man, you don't want to engage *me* in locker room tactics. I *am* the master."

"I am sure you are," David said in a soft sensual voice. He knew Barry was going to put him through the wringer today. He might as well flirt with him now to throw him off his game.

Barry was gay, married to his first (and last Barry always said) husband for twenty years. Before that he was a loving husband and father. It hadn't been simple to come out in Minnesota with a wife and two kids. He had taken almost 15 years to work up to it.

David met Barry at Brooks Brothers when David moved back to Palm Beach to work in Dr. Ma's practice. Since then the two had an annual tradition of cleaning out David's closet of shoes, clothes, accessories and household furnishings. Ostensibly it was for charity. David knew for Barry, it was also to keep David on the edge of fashion.

Dr. Ma had Winnie, her friend and assistant who had come from retail to maintain her closet and an interior decorator friend to redo her furnishings annually. Dr. Ma also had a strong fashion sense. David, not so much.

Barry could not understand how a man as stunning as David, and obviously bi-sexual if you believed the rumors, could be so fashion sense deprived. "You must be overwhelming your natural gay fashion gene with too much heterosexual exposure," he called after David as he walked away to get dressed for the day.

"I am not gay, straight, nor bi-sexual," David called back over his shoulder. As he walked away, he removed the towels from around his waist and shoulders and tossed both into the bathroom as he passed. Barry had an excellent view of the younger man's powerful back, legs, and buttocks before he disappeared into his bedroom. "I am an opportunist."

"You are going to give an old man a heart attack," Barry called back. "Please put something on before you come back this way. You are the most gorgeous thing I have ever seen outside of a, well I was going to say, a magazine, but I think I may be underselling you."

David laughed from the room down the hall. "Come on back if you want to get started on the closet clean out," he teased. "I'm not shy."

"You *are* evil," Barry said, chuckling. "I know you are just getting your licks in before I spend the day teasing you unmercifully. We are having a small dinner tonight at our place, I expect to be done with you by then."
"Am I invited?" David asked, walking back into the room, fully dressed.

"Of course," Barry answered. "Don even invited your little girlfriend so you won't feel over whelmed by all the gay male energy."

"What girlfriend?" David asked, his eyebrows drawing together in a slight frown.

"The McCarthy girl," Barry answered over his shoulder as he walked out the front door to get David going on the day.

David's phone buzzed in his pocket before he could answer. He followed Barry down the narrow stone stairs reading the text from Dr. Ma. Apparently they had a new murder to help Detective Brenner investigate.

"And I thought the day wasn't going to be completely weird," David muttered to himself. He joined Barry on the sidewalk in the wall to wall Florida sunlight that came with Summer.

Barry utilized a small sun umbrella to block the damage to his skin and complexion. He didn't offer to share with David. He knew he would get turned down. The younger man had the glowing tight skin of every aesthetician's dream. How he kept it that way was beyond Barry's understanding.

He knew David ran every day in the bright sunlight of the South Florida morning. He also knew every drop of skincare product he left with him last year would be untouched in the bottles he would replace in David's bathroom. Never let it be said he didn't do his job if David suddenly started sporting wrinkles.

"I see you look as perfect as last year this time," Barry said, bending forward to inspect David in the bright sunlight. "Not a hint of a wrinkle, flawless muscle, and you just glow. Must be all those damn plants you eat."

David smiled and laughed. "Have I passed inspection?" he inquired.

"Not until I see you completely naked while the tailor is fitting you today. I am, of course, looking for signs of aging. Love handles, sagging skin and so forth." Barry smiled at him lasciviously.

"I am pretty sure the tailor doesn't need me to strip naked to get my measurements," David said, narrowing his eyes at his friend. "You got away with that once, when I didn't know any better."

"No reason to change the tradition now then," Barry said, leading the way towards Worth Avenue, his sun umbrella held high.

David shook his head, smiling and followed him. "You have a couple hours before I need to have lunch," he warned.

"That is another thing," Barry said, falling back to walk companionably side by side. David was a good three inches taller at 6'5" but Barry just held the umbrella lower to avoid poking him in the eye. "How do you consume the vast amounts of food you do and stay so slim? It can't be all the exercise!"

"You want to believe it isn't the exercise because you hate to sweat and that it isn't what I eat because you love cheese and meat," David teased.

"Oh, now you are sounding like Dr. Ma," Barry said. "Don't get all preachy on me. Tell me something like you burn it off having sex every night for hours."

David shook his head in the negative. "That is definitely not the way I burn off calories. I wish it were."

Barry rolled his eyes and stopped to turn into Versace. "So now I have to get you laid as well?"

"Could you?" David teased.

"Who needs to get laid?" the perfectly attired store manager said, walking up to Barry and giving him a quick kiss on both cheeks. The beautiful young woman laughed and looked at David. "Not you? I know Barry is taken."

David flushed slightly. "Barry's idea, not mine really. I am happy being celibate. Gives me more energy to work out." He walked towards the back of the store as the tiny Italian tailor walked out and waved him in.

"Seriously?" the young woman said to Barry. "Okay, what is wrong with him? Nobody that looks like that can't get laid. Especially on the Island. Is he a freak? A serial killer?" Her brunette hair fell in shimmering locks to her waist. Flawlessly painted skin concealed what could be a less than perfect complexion. The tightly fitted sheath dress, showed her uber thin, Palm Beach figure.

"Who is a serial killer?" a heavy Italian accent preceded the small shop owner. He walked up to Barry and gave him a more enthusiastic version of the cheek kisses he had received from the female manager. "My friend! Did you bring that young male model you drag around

58

every year before we all mange to close for the Season?"

"He is a model?" the manger said, her interest peaking.

"No dear," Barry said. "Vincenzo is pulling your leg. David is an acupuncture physician right here in West Palm Beach. He has an apartment over by Renato's and gobs of family money. He is also single and mostly celibate because he is shy and we are thinking, closeted bisexual. Go make a play for him before we leave for the next couture shop. Maybe you will get lucky."

The pretty woman laughed, but headed back towards the tailor's area. "And so it begins," Vincenzo laughed, slapping Barry on the back. "You do this to him every year. It is fun to watch, no?"

"Yes it is," Barry agreed. "It takes him months to sort out all the phone numbers and invitations he gets in one day shopping with me. It's fun for you too, because he drops a bundle here."

"True!" his friend laughed. "I put several things aside for you to decide on for him. It must be enjoyable, no? To play dress up with such a beautiful toy. I still remember the first year when

you told him he had to strip down for the tailor to get the right measurements."
Barry was laughing, tears coming to his eyes now. "I am surprised he still trusts me."

"I am surprised he still employs you!" Vincenzo said. "Come, I have biscotti," he said motioning to the back. "Cappuccino? You can sit and watch Miranda give your boy a hard time."

From the look David gave Barry when he arrived in the back, the older man could tell Miranda was living up to his expectations. The stunning younger man was standing on the tailor's platform in a soon to be perfectly fitted pair of tropical wool dress pants. Just enough fabric weight and a touch of spandex made sure every asset would be well represented.

Barry ran his hands over the matching jacket that was hanging on the wall pegs. "Beautiful," he commented.

"Yes," Miranda said smiling, her eyes on David's shirtless figure. She held a crisp white dress shirt in one hand. "Already pinned up," she smiled. "No reason to leave it on him. He could get stuck. Nice tattoos," she almost purred.

David had a unique array of tattoos across his lower abdomen and pelvis. Vines and leaves branched from the main ones on his hips and spread across his buttocks. From there they dove down below the close fitting black briefs he wore. Barry knew they wrapped around his butt cheeks.

Nobody Barry knew had any idea what the tattoos represented and David wasn't open to questions about them. The lower abdomen pattern had slivers of gems under thin layers of skin. A friend of Barry's deeply into tattooing had never seen anything like them from the description. He still wanted Barry to talk David into showing them to him one day.

David was just slipping off the slacks for the tailor when Vincenzo arrived with the coffee and biscotti. "Did you know they found a body this morning? Here in Palm Beach?" he asked, looking at David pointedly. "Don't you and your colleague help the police in these matters?"

David took an espresso from the tray and answered Vincenzo in flawless Italian. Several minutes later, with Miranda translating as best she could, Barry understood that yes, David knew and yes, Dr. Ma and he helped.

"I will never understand how five minutes of gabbing produces nothing in context," Barry said. He was referring to the length of David and Vincenzo's conversation in Italian.

David grinned. "Because so much else, other than the topic you started on, is being said. Conversational versus informational Barry, think of it that way."

"Okay, you really have to stop sounding so much like Dr. Ma today. Try being the shy, overwhelmed young man, made worse by my intense sexual harassment of you via shop owners and their staff, that you are every year."

"What a mouthful," David began, holding up a finger to stop Barry's retort. "I did not just say that. You are off to a roaring start today my friend." David jerked his chin at Miranda's retreating figure. "If she could have gotten rid of the tailor, I think I would have been in trouble."

"Right," Barry said. "Enough about you, tell us all about the murder!"

They asked Vincenzo to join them after they made a quick stop at Brooks Brothers, but the busy little man couldn't get away from the shop.

"Tell me everything later," he said to Barry. Winking at David, he waved good bye.

Another stop at Barry's former employer added two pair of tailored chinos and two pull over sweaters for David. "Are you sure that was all?" he asked the older man, laughing.

"Yes," Barry sniffed. "I am getting other items for you elsewhere this year. I want to change your style a bit." John, the current manager rolled his eyes at the comment.

The two friends walked west along Worth Avenue. Their packages would be delivered to David's apartment later. Except for David's outfit Barry's picked out for dinner that evening. They hung it in Barry's car parked on Peruvian.

David waited until they were seated at Renato's for lunch. "What information about the murder did you get from Vincenzo at Ferragamo and John at Brooks Brothers?" he asked.

David knew there would be two more hours of shopping after lunch. Plenty of time to gather even more gossip. Then they would finally be done for the day.

"The buzz is that Barry Cohen's fifth wife was found dead on the beach this morning. Nude!" Barry said.

"She was actually found on a beach house roof in the 800 block of South Ocean Ave," David corrected, frowning slightly. They sat away from anyone and kept their voices down. No need adding more fuel to the fire going around the island about the murder.

"So she was just lying there on the tile roof?" Barry said, his hand half covering his mouth in an expression of surprise. "How awful!"

"Did you know her?" David answered. He almost took back the question as soon as it left his lips. After years in Palm Beach, and with the older man's outgoing personality, Barry knew everyone.

"Of course!" Barry returned. "She was the new young wife of an older man in Palm Beach. They shop! Do you think you are my only client? They have a penthouse in that new building off 5th Avenue in Manhattan, and a house here in Palm Beach."

"I'm sure you have many clients. She apparently won't be needing you next season," David replied.

The waiter brought their pre-ordered meal almost as soon as they sat down. David tucked into a large and fragrant bowl of lightly steamed vegetables with fresh herbs and a light toss of vinegar and olive oil. Even Barry had to admit it smelled delicious.

Taking measured spoonfuls of his lentil soup, Barry thought for a moment. "I shopped for her last year. She was still trying to get her footing in Town. It is not the same as being in Manhattan."

"The last time anyone saw her was at a penthouse apartment in Manhattan after some big party," David said.

"Let a murder occur in this Town with a resident, young fifth wife or not, and tongues will wag," Barry said. "Kill a prostitute and leave her in the middle of A1A like what happened 20 years ago and you will never hear about it unless you have an inside line at the police department."

"It won't even be there if you Google about murders that occurred in the Town proper," David said thoughtfully. "Because it didn't of course. Socialite murder yes, common prostitute, no. Must have happened in West Palm Beach."

"I assume you and Dr. Ma are going to help with this one?" Barry asked around a bite of pasta. He was almost addicted to the gluten free pasta bowl tossed with garlic, spinach and olive oil.

"Of course," David answered, watching his friend enjoy his food. David had wiped out the plate of veggies they brought him and was letting it digest. Despite his habit of rapidly finishing a meal, he seemed to suffer no digestive issues. Perhaps it was the fact he ate mostly raw or slightly steamed veggies.

"You never really told me how you two got so involved with helping the police solve crimes," Barry said, pausing to sip his glass of wine. Only one glass with lunch, but tonight was the dinner party and several more glasses awaited him there.

"It is pretty much Dr. Ma's thing," David answered. He looked up to see Detective

Jeremy Brenner walking towards them, smiling. "Here comes the reason, I believe."

Brenner shook hands with both men and sat down to join them. His pre-ordered meal also appeared within moments. "How is the soup?" he asked Barry.

"Delicious as always," came the answer. Barry looked him over appraisingly. "David and I are doing a bit of shopping today Detective, I could help you update your wardrobe too?"

Brenner laughed. "I would love to dress like David does Barry," he said. "Problem is, one of his suits will cover my car payments for the year."

David flushed slightly. He was always uncomfortable with the vast amount of money he had at his disposal. Changing his wardrobe every year was more about the charitable donation of his old things and to keep Dr.Ma and Barry happy that he was not a fashion faux pas.

"If you will come with us and take some of the heat off me, I will gladly pay for your clothes," David offered.

Brenner smiled at him. "Yes, I hear that Barry does his best to drive you crazy by introducing you to every eligible young woman or man in retail once a year. Lucky dog."

"Right," David said. "Not exactly lucky, harassed is more like it. I do fine on my own. Barry thinks I work and train more than I socialize He doesn't realize I have limited success dating. No matter who introduces me."

Brenner paused, remembering the debacle with Karen McCarthy last year. "Yeah, like Karen, I am sorry about that."

"Karen McCarthy? She recently told me she and David had a thing going so I would invite her to the party tonight," Barry said.

Brenner looked at him then at David. "What is she up to with that I wonder?" he said.

"Exactly my thoughts," David nodded.

Barry looked at both handsome young men sitting with him. "First, I have to spend more time with gorgeous young men," he thought. "Second, I can't believe both of them are unattached. What is this world coming to?"

Aloud he said. "Tonight should be interesting then."

"We are headed to Hermes after lunch, then Ralph Lauren," David said looking at Jeremy carefully. He seriously doubted the 'all business' cop would join them.

"As much as I would like to, I can't. I assume I will see you and Dr. Ma tomorrow about the new case?" Brenner asked.

"She is already on it today," David replied. "The murder is all over the Avenue in the gossip grapevine by the way."

Brenner raised his eyebrows. "Great!" he said. "Let me know what is being said. You never know when someone will have information for me. If you are talking about the case while you two shop, I have to take back all the time wasting thoughts I was laying on you."

David grinned. "This is hands down the most tortuous day of my year and you are giving me a hard time?"

Brenner laughed and took his wallet out to pay for his lunch. David shook his head in the negative. "Let me Jeremy, please. It would be my pleasure."

The detective nodded his thanks. He always forgot what a generous person David was. "The man never seems to miss a chance to give some of what he has," he thought.

He knew that his martial arts teacher lived as simple a life as possible. Both he and Dr. Ma were very active philanthropists in Town. The clothing Barry provided for David was needed to keep up with his social obligations. Jeremy did not suffer from many social obligations needing fashionable clothing.

Brenner smiled as he left. "Gentlemen," he said.

"Detective," Barry responded. David just smiled.

"You know," Barry said to David. "That man would kill in the right clothes."

David laughed. "Keep working on him Barry," he said. "Maybe for the Policeman's Ball this season."

"I will charge it to your account," Barry said as they left the restaurant to finish their day.

"Anytime," David agreed softly. "Anytime."

Chapter Four - The Dinner Party

David and Barry finished their shopping trip too late to drop David off at home. Barry took him straight to his condo for the dinner party. Don greeted them at the door, already fussing.

"Caterers are here, everything is almost ready, where have you two been?" all came out in a rush.

"Relax Don," Barry said. "Everything is on track. It is just a casual get together."

Don rolled his eyes at David. "If you could see the bill you wouldn't call it casual. What are you wearing?" he said taking in David's polo shirt and khaki shorts. "Did he drag you here without letting you change?"

"David's clothes for the evening are here," Barry said handing the recently steamed Ralph Lauren chinos and button down shirt to him. "The belt from Hermes is in the bag with delicates. Those shoes are fine. David use the shower in the guest room before Don has a fit."

Knowing to remain quiet and disappear was the best course of action for the next half hour. David headed for the shower. He could hear the two older men chattering excitedly behind him. They loved to throw their dinner parties.

Remembering that Karen was coming made him pause. No time to ask Barry more about her now. "I wonder what she is up to now," he thought.

In an hour, the elegant apartment was filling with gay men. Couples and singles, all were friends of Barry and Don. David sat quietly while they greeted each other and mingled. Karen arrived after everyone else.

"He's mine gentlemen," Karen said with a dramatic wave of her hand. She swept in to the intimate gathering and sat in David's lap. "Hands off."

David looked at her in almost comical surprise. His mouth opened then closed without uttering a sound. He was really at a loss for words based on the fact they hadn't even spoken since their return from the ill fated South Africa trip, months ago.

The small array of guests from Barry's party all laughed at her dramatic entrance and returned to their conversation. Don came over to rescue

David. He sat down next to him on the living room couch.

"So David," Don said. "How is the practice going? I understand from Dr. Ma you are taking separate doctoral studies classes once a month."

David leaned around Karen's figure to answer. She was half draped on his lap and upper body, her arm around his neck. "Tough," he said. "The week I am gone every month, Dr. Ma has to pick up the slack in patient care. I have a one month break coming up soon."

"What about the martial arts school?" Barry said, joining them and handing Karen a glass of wine. David was sure the last thing Karen needed was another drink before dinner. From her behavior and breath, David was assuming she had started on the evening's alcohol imbibing early.

"Oooh," Stuart, one of the guests said in a slightly flirty tone. He came over and sat on the other side of David. The Rochebobois designed three seater was feeling a bit claustrophobic in the center with Karen on David's lap and a man on either side. "Is that how you stay in such amazing shape?"

David flushed slightly. It seemed he had been successfully avoiding attention until now. He wasn't sure if Karen's arrival was beneficial to take the interest off him or not. Not, he decided as she bent forward and planted a lingering, wine flavored kiss on his mouth.

Again, temporarily speechless at her behavior, David said nothing. Karen answered for him. "That is just one of the things he does to stay in such amazing shape," she almost purred. "Have you had the pleasure of seeing him naked?"

David looked at Barry for help. The older man just shook his head and laughed. "You are on your own there buddy," he replied. "Besides, this is beyond interesting."

Stuart was grinning ear to ear, his husband Mike was now standing behind the spot Stuart was seated in, looking at David sympathetically. His look seems to say, "When they are drunk, they are a handful."

David finally came to his own defense. "No, they have *not* seen me naked, and neither have you, really." He was trying to extract himself from Karen's half embrace gracefully, without being thought of as a jerk.

"Well we can rectify that," Stuart said slyly. "Right here is fine with me. How about you Karen?"

Just as David was about to protest, the chef Don and Barry hired for the intimate evening meal came out to announce that dinner was being served.

Barry grabbed Karen's hand and pulled her up off of David's lap. "Let me escort you my dear," he said, giving David a 'you owe me' look over his shoulder.

"You are the one who invited her," David mumbled softly as they walked away. He got up and walked in with Stuart and Mike.

Mike put his hand on David's shoulder and said, "Stuart is just teasing you David. You know what a flirt he is. But the young lady seems out for something more than that. Isn't that your girlfriend? I thought Barry said he invited your girlfriend?"

"I don't have a girlfriend," David said exasperatedly.

"Boyfriend then?" Frank, another guest who had come alone said walking up behind them.

"I'm not seeing anyone," David answered honestly.

"Oh that was a mistaken confession," Mike said rolling his eyes.
Frank raised his hand in the air and pointed at David. In a loud voice he announced to the room of gay men, "Fair game!"

"What?" David said, blushing deeply now.

"I told you that was a mistake," Mike grinned.

"Hands off the big guy," Don said. He slipped his arm around David's shoulders and steered him to the end of the table. At 6'4", Don was closest to David's height. "Here, sit with me at this end. I will protect you from the vultures."

"Thanks," David said. "Things are a bit out of hand with Karen. I think she's trashed. After dinner, someone needs to get her home. She shouldn't be driving."

"You are nominated," Don said smiling.

"I was trying to avoid that," David said, looking down the table to where Karen sat next to Barry. She was staring back at him.

"Boy, you and I have to have a sit down on missing opportunities," Don laughed, reverting momentarily to his soft southern drawl.

David looked at him seriously. "I don't think this is a particularly good opportunity for me. We almost had a thing several times and crash landed before take off. Each time. Then she just started seeing a friend who is a cop here on the island. I'm not sure if that is still going on now."

"Detective Brenner?" Don asked.

"Yes," David said. "Jeremy is a friend. It was awkward at first, but Karen and I haven't even spoken since. Then she shows up tonight all over me. Who told Barry she was my girlfriend?"

"She did," Don answered. "At my shop." Don owned a high end antique shop off of Worth Avenue. "She and Barry have been chummy for awhile. She told him that you two were hot and heavy when she wrangled an invitation to our dinner tonight."

David looked at him confused. "I have no idea why she would do that. Really, we never got anything going together."

Don looked at him for a moment and then said, "Don't worry about it. Enjoy dinner and we will work things out later who takes the inebriated female home. There isn't one guy here who would *want* to number one, and number two, all of them would be trustworthy to get her there safely."

The dinner was being served by the chef and his assistant. Muted candlelight glowed on the table that was set like an typical Summer seafood fest in the Hamptons.

Freshly steamed shellfish was heaped in piles around deep bowls for cast offs. A large central platter boasted steamed vegetables. Smaller bowls held melted butter and various dipping sauces. Fragrant crusty rolls were piled in linen lined wicker baskets.

Ever the thoughtful hosts, Barry and Don arranged for David to be given a platter of raw fresh veggies, nuts and seeds. His preferred fare. Fresh fruit awaited him for dessert while the rest of the guests would indulge in a melt in your mouth strawberry shortcake.

Barry and Don had a third floor condo in a five story ocean front building off of A1A. The building was built in 2010 from the shell of a much older structure. The new manifestation was modern and roomy. Each residence boasted both an East and West view of the respective waterways.

As a peninsular shaped island, Palm Beach could offer unobstructed views of both the Atlantic ocean and the Intracoastal Waterway on some of the more narrow sections. The large, open, central living space extended onto a deep balcony where the Hampton-esque dining table and chairs had been set up.

The interior of the modern apartment was open and flowing. Sleek modern furniture in revisited 1950's styling was strategically placed for comfort and style.

Frank, sitting next to David, gave him a broad smile. "Vegan?" he inquired, flashing a set of gleaming white teeth.Close enough to David's height. At six foot two inches tall, Frank didn't have to look up very far to meet the blue eyes of the stunning man next to him.

A daily two hour workout ritual kept Frank fit and muscled. His slender frame allowed his expensive clothing to drape easily around broad shoulders and a narrow waist.

David caught himself looking appraisingly at his dinner companion when Frank said. "If you like what you see, we could arrange a private showing later," His gleaming smile became somewhat lascivious.

David blushed and looked away from the handsome man next to him. "No, really, I'm sorry," he stumbled, finally recovering himself. "I was just admiring your, I mean wondering," he stopped and took a deep breath. "I was wondering what sport you played. You look very fit. I have a practice in Sports Medicine."

Frank's smile widened even further. "Hmmm, sport? That depends on what you consider a sport." He put his hand on David's arm. Barry, circulating around the table to talk, leaned down between them and removed Frank's hand. David flushed slightly. The direction of the conversation was clear.

"Oh no you don't Frank," Barry said. "David is not even vaguely prepared to engage you in *conversation*, much less anything else. He is genuinely innocent of your perverted lifestyle."

Several of the men at the table laughed, while Karen glowered from the other end. "Oh stop," Stuart said to her. "We all got the message you tried to deliver, except the man you were trying to claim seemed to be in the dark! Give it up for now girl and enjoy dinner. Either Frank will win him to the dark side, or he will be available for you to drag home!"

Karen threw a roll at him and another round of laughter came from the dinner guests. David just looked at Barry. "I'm sorry big guy," Barry said. "I should never have invited her. You are getting it from both sides tonight."

"Such an idea!" Stuart said. Mike took the opportunity to stuff a grilled shrimp in his spouse's mouth.

"Enough," Mike said. "Leave David alone and let him eat his dinner in peace. Besides, the word is that you're bisexual David. True?"

David met the curious glances around him and answered truthfully, as he always did. "More celibate than bisexual really."

"Oh no, he did *not* just say that," Frank laughed.

"Enough!" Barry said and looked at David. "Eat. If your mouth is busy with my delicious food, you won't say anything further to provoke them."

He hadn't touched the food in front of him yet. Nearly unheard of for the always hungry Tiger. David was feeling anxious about the whole situation at dinner. He didn't mind the flirting from Frank or any of Barry's gay male friends. It was Karen's off the wall behavior. She hadn't been herself after returning from the South African trip.

David knew Dr. Ma had met with their solicitor, Allistair McGowan today to discuss taking on the responsibility of Karen's *Save the Tiger's Foundation*. Her father Joseph, had contacted Dr. Ma about them taking over the charitable fund.

"Apparently Karen is no longer interested in running the charity," Ma had explained to him. "Do you want to take it over?"

David had immediately agreed. Any tiger based charity was personal for him. When Karen and he were in South Africa a few months ago visiting the Luohu Reserve, he had been overwhelmed by the raw beauty of the area.

Except for the attack on their bush camp, the dead bodies, and Karen never talking to him again after they got back, it had been a good trip.

More fragrant and steaming dishes were set down and the food settled everyone into happy conversation. Even Karen. David relaxed and ate his meal while chatting wth Stuart across from him, Don on one side and Frank on the other. The soft navy sky of the South Florida evening draped over the water outside of the condo patio.

Frank was a local real estate guru and Stuart was a well know dance instructor. Stuart's husband Mike, seated next to Stuart, was a movie producer. Mostly indie films about the environment. Mike said that he and Angelina Jolie were collaborating on some project about educating African children displaced by civil war.

Waves gently crashed on the beach and guests got up from the table after dinner to wander around the condo, chatting. David walked towards the balcony. Polished aluminum poles held blue plexiglass panels in a mostly see through modernistic barrier to the ocean side.

Leaning his six foot five inch tall frame against the four foot high barrier, David watched the full moon leave a broad swath along the ocean from its perch in the night sky. It seemed like a silvery carpet from the silvery globe to the sandy beach.

"Beautiful," Frank's voice said suddenly from beside him. David had been so lost in thought and relaxed, he missed the man settling in beside him.
"Stunning view," David agreed.

"Yes," Frank said. David realized the other man was looking at him intensely and standing close enough to touch. Frank put his hand on David's shoulder. Shifting to create more space between them, David smiled uncomfortably.

"Look, Frank," he began. "I am good with getting to know you better, but I am out of my depth if you are interested in a hookup for the evening."

"I just wanted to discuss the comment you made at dinner about being celibate," Frank said, laughing softly. "That is such a shame."

The handsome realtor leaned closer, David could smell the alcohol on his breath. "Is everyone drunk tonight?" he thought. At charitable functions he expected it, he was surprised by it at a small get together. As Frank slipped his hand off David's shoulder and down his back and buttocks, David put a hand out to push him back.

Then he heard a loud crack overhead.

David looked up to see a large stone vase on the upstairs' neighbor's balcony tip suddenly in his direction. The balconies were staggered, so each progressive one was about halfway in from the one below. The higher you went in the building, the fewer apartments. The whole thing finished with one large, top floor penthouse.

It took him a moment to react. Frank was close enough to brush his lips over David's cheek as he turned his face to look up. The stone vase was about three feet high. It broke loose from where it seemed to have been cemented and shot straight towards them.

David grabbed Frank in his powerful arms and pulled them both backwards over the balcony rail. He heard a scream as someone else saw the flying stone projectile. Then the crash came from it breaking through the plexiglass barrier.

David tried to transition to his Elemental Tiger form as they dropped, but things were moving too quickly. He heard a crack when he landed under Frank on the balcony floor below. Probably his ribcage from how it felt. Rolling sideways, Frank held tightly in his arms, he heard the vase land just after they did. Fragments of stone shattered and sprayed over the balcony and them.

He let Frank go and rose to his feet in a second, ready to fight. He knew the vase hadn't accidentally fallen and he didn't know what he was up against. The pain in his side made him bite his lip to keep from groaning aloud. Definitely cracked ribs from the fall. They would heal, but they hurt like hell for now.

Apart from the screaming above him and the quiet of the empty apartment whose balcony they had landed on, David saw and sensed nothing. He bent over to help Frank up. The man was completely dazed. David had kept him from all but slight cuts from the stone fragments.

The front apartment door, in a direct line from the patio, suddenly burst open. David stiffened for a fight despite the pain. Seeing who had opened the apartment allowed him to relax somewhat. It was Barry. David's tiger instinct was still making him look around warily.

Barry came rushing though the empty apartment towards them. David could hear sirens in the background getting closer. He suddenly realized he was no longer standing but rather kneeling on the stone fragments, spitting blood out of his mouth.

"Okay," he thought. "A little in shock from the fall." Then his vision dimmed slightly.

"Oh my god David, are you alright?" Barry said in a panicked voice.

"Great," he thought. "How bad was this injury really? Heal, he commanded his body." A wave of dizziness made him put a hand out to steady himself from collapsing.

Frank had recovered himself enough to now kneel down and wrap an arm around David. He tried to help him up. He was rewarded with a grunt of pain from the younger man. He did not realize he was pressing on a few fresh rib fractures.

"Sorry!" he said, unwrapping his arm. "Oh god, are you okay? What the hell happened?"

"I tried to keep us from being crushed by a loose vase from the apartment above Barry's," David said through slightly clenched teeth. The pain was getting better, but slowly.

Getting a nod from David that he was going to be okay, Barry had looked around the patio briefly and rushed back to the front door of the empty apartment to guide the Palm Beach Fire Department inside.

The first medic to reach him was the pretty woman from the last time he had been injured in Palm Beach. She immediately recognized him. "You?" she said. Do you try to get yourself killed on a regular basis?"

She helped him up to lean against some stable patio furniture after her assessment. "I'm fine," David told her. Blood was still dripping from his mouth. A quick check with his tongue found a deep gash inside his mouth from his teeth. "Nothing more serious," he thought. "Except the broken ribs."

Police and Firefighters seemed to be everywhere, checking out the scene and the damage. Don came down just as the pretty medic was reluctantly clearing David from any life threatening injury. "I can't believe you are not seriously injured after that fall," she said to him. "You should let us take you to the hospital for a complete exam."

He looked at her more closely. At just five foot six inches tall, he towered over her. Her blond hair was pulled back professionally into a bun at the back of her head. Light blue eyes stared back at him. Her name tag said 'James.'

She was holding the release form he had asked for as if she didn't want to give it to him. He took it and signed his name. She looked disappointed. "That is my cell phone," David said pointing to the number on the form. He wouldn't be so presumptuous as to ask for *her* number. "Please use it if I can buy you a cup of coffee sometime. I am not always bleeding and on death's door."

The pretty medic opened her mouth in surprise but didn't say anything as she turned away. "She seems normal," David thought. "I could do with some normal these days."

Frank walked over to him after the medics finished having him sign a release. David noticed that Frank hadn't said anything about falling *with* him over the balcony, or what he was trying to do before they fell. Frank had a few scratches that could have come from any involvement in the scenario.

Dr. Ma was the next person David saw. He had healed for the most part while the medic was fussing over him. Gritting his teeth when she palpated the area of the fractured ribs kept her from knowing how much pain he was in.

He reached out mentally towards Dr. Ma, but the Dragon's mind was closed to him. They would talk later. Stuart came rushing over to him, chattering a mile a minute. "All that martial arts training," he was saying. "Incredible! You two could have been killed. You look like you just landed holding Frank on top of you. Like a superhero!"

"I know some producers who would have killed to have gotten that on film," Mike said, arriving behind Stuart.

David smiled despite the gravity of the situation. They were excited he and Frank had lived. He wanted to know who tried to kill them. Dr. Ma looked his way. He knew she could hear his thoughts.

Detective Brenner was the last person in the door of the empty apartment. "What are you doing here?" David teased him with a slight grimace. "Nobody died."

"Ha ha," Brenner said, looking not at all like he was being funny. "I can't leave you unattended apparently. You need to move out of my jurisdiction if you are going to opt for something like this on a regular basis. I have a case to work already, let's not add another."

Walking slowly out of the rubble strewn patio, David sat on the living room couch in the empty apartment. Dr. Ma came and sat next to him. Frank joined them and introduced himself to her. "Are you alright?" she asked Frank solicitously.

"Thanks to David I am," he answered. Getting up to leave, he looked at the beautiful woman sitting on the couch next to his recent dinner companion. "Hope to see you both again sometime soon. Good night."

Chapter Five - The Body on the Roof

They were sitting in David's apartment after Dr. Ma drove him home. Dr. Ma and David had stayed long enough to make sure Barry and Don were okay. The caterers had cleaned up and taken everything from the party. Most of the debris was on the patio of their downstairs neighbor.

The firefighters had contacted building maintenance and a plywood panel replaced the broken plexiglass barrier section. There wasn't even damage to Barry and Don's patio, per se. Only the panel the vase hit, was broken out and in pieces on the floor below.

The guests all left as soon as they were allowed. All left instructions for their hosts to call them if they needed anything, of course. What could you need? Nobody had been seriously injured. Except David. This would be the talk of the Town for some time. Party of the year!

Nidi, David's house djinn, was fussing over him and muttering under her breath. She had taken off his shirt and pants and was trying to get him to go and get in the shower.

Djinn had magical skills. Unfortunately, she was not present when David was injured this evening. She was totally devoted to him after a millennia in his service. Kaia, the ancient Earth mother had given her to him when he was created.

Dr. Ma laughed at her ministrations. "Go on," she said to David. "Nidi is right, I'm following." Ma had given him a good once over for any un-healing injuries when Nidi had taken off with his clothing.

"Did you transition?" Dr. Ma asked him. She hadn't asked him anything up until now. They had a uncomfortable silence between them during the trip home from the dinner party.

"No," David said looking at her. "It felt like, well I tried, but it happened too fast." David remembered the first time she had taught him to resist transforming in less than optimal circumstances.
He hadn't been stronger when she adopted him this time around. He never was. He seemed to acquire new skills at an extremely slow rate and lose most of them every time he died.

"Good thing," Ma said smiling.

"You've taught me well," he laughed. "No seriously, I don't know how that would have worked out."

"Well, you wouldn't have cracked a few ribs for sure," Ma laughed. She stopped, looking at him seriously. "You felt nothing? No Otherworldly presence?"

"No," he said slowly, then flushed slightly. "I was, ah, distracted."

"Hmm?" Ma commented, raising her eyebrows. "I will have to meet this distraction. And at Barry's party? You are opening your options?"

"Not exactly," David said , his cheeks deepening in color. "I need to stick with my plan of training, working, eating and repeating. Keeps me out of trouble."

"Hardly," Dr. Ma smiled. "I heard Barry say Karen was there, but I didn't see her."

"She was there before and during dinner," David said, frowning slightly. "A bit drunk and acting strangely. I didn't see her after dinner because I was busy falling off the patio and making a mess of the downstairs apartment."

"Well done though, nobody died," Ma said, lips pursed like she was debating something. "I wanted to discuss Jeremy's murder case if you are up to it."

David had washed up quickly while they were talking. His shower enclosure was completely open to the bathroom with a free standing glass panel. He stepped onto the bath mat and toweled off. Nidi handed him a pair of old sweat pants and a T-shirt. Barry hadn't gotten rid of those items. David had had to hide them. They walked back out to his living room.

"Shoot," David said, encouraging her to talk. He got comfortable on his new, Thayer Coggin, classic design couch. Dr. Ma settled in to the Origami chair and ottoman from the same designer.

"Barry's choices?" Ma said, running her hand over the chair's fabric.

"Yes," David smiled. "I liked the old furniture, but it will benefit whatever charity he earmarked it for, and Allistair's accountant Christa will be happy to take the deduction for us."

Nidi returned with a tray of drinks and snacks. Sparkling water for both with an array of David's raw bars wasn't much, but she tried.

Ma had recently given her a forced vacation in the alternate dimension where she and Allistair kept their reference library. The true Library of Alexandria.

The ancient creature seemed completely revitalized now that she was back. Ma remembered her sleeping most of her days away before her time away. Sleeping instead of taking care of David and his apartment.

"Thank you Nidi," he said. "I will be fine for the rest of the night."

Nidi gave him a doubtful look and drifted off to attend to David's collection of Vanda orchids.

His apartment, between Worth Avenue and Peruvian, had floor to ceiling windows in century old stone walls. The wood floors gleamed as if nobody had ever walked on them. Nidi carefully spread a large cloth below each window before misting the hanging plants with David's special mixture.

The soft rustling plant speak drifted through the quiet space as the orchids thanked the little Djinn for taking care of them. Purples, pinks, yellows and green flowers seemed to bloom on the large plants all days of the year.

"She is doing well," Ma commented, indicating Nidi.

"Yes," David agreed. "I think Maia did more than just let her rest and recover in the Library."

Maia was the official librarian. She had volunteered for the job when Allistair and Dr. Ma created the location over two millennia ago. Lover of Zeus and mother of Hermes, Maia was a beautiful, if retiring, daughter of the Titan Atlas.

"So," Dr. Ma began. "You received my text?"

"Yes," David replied nodding. "Why do humans kill each other at such a rate?"

"Human killer with Otherworldly assistance," Dr. Ma corrected him.

David should have known Detective Brenner wouldn't need their help for a plain old run of the mill murder involving only human participants.

"Jeremy was with me, as you saw, when the Spirit Wind vision came," Ma began. It was the woman whose body he found this morning. She must have died and released her Spirit in or around Palm Beach."

"I saw you and Jeremy on the bench," David said. "You will have to tell me how that happened. Weren't you just coming back from the night ride?"

"I was," she said. "The vision came to me while I was riding into West Palm over the Okeechobee bridge. I stopped to sit on a bench and let it come, when Jeremy flagged me down to tell me about the call from NYPD,"

David grinned. "Seriously? Things are getting too weird these days."

"Weird?" Dr. Ma asked. "Was that our teaching assistant wrapped around you in the Clinic's hallway I saw?" She raised her eyebrows questioningly. "How did that happen exactly?"

David flushed. "He followed me in from the dojo and I couldn't get rid of him before the strength of the vision hit me. It was fast."

"What does he think happened?" Dr. Ma asked.

"Low blood sugar," David said. "I took him to dinner before he drove me home."

"He must have been thrilled," she smiled. "On a more serious note, he is crazy about you. You have to put a stop to that."

"I know," David said unhappily. "Let's stick with the murder right now. I will handle Sosam."

Ma gave him a long searching look. When David said nothing further on the subject of their teaching assistant, she continued telling him about the case.

"Jeremy said she was splayed out on the roof of that small beach house in the 800 block of Ocean Avenue. You know, right where North County meets at the water. When the sun started to bloat her, people noticed she was dead, and not sunbathing," Ma said.

"Ugh," David commented. "Who found her?"

"Terry and Sam were running together," she replied.

"Good thing it was them," he said. "Terry is mister observant. She might have been there a lot longer if it was up to someone else to notice."

"I think Terry and Sam are not particularly happy they were so observant," Ma replied. I told them to meet us for lunch tomorrow at the clinic. A couple of energy balancing sessions are in order."

"Sounds good," David agreed. "You can pull some details out of their memories while you are 'balancing' them."

"Exactly," she agreed. "I need to go the scene tonight and see if I can get a trail on who transported the victim to the rooftop. She was frozen David. I think she died from that. Then they left her there and she started to thaw. Willing to go with me?"

In answer, David stood up and walked back to his bedroom. Appearing moments later in training gear, he said, "I'm ready. Do you want to change?"

Ma nodded and went to pull her spare black training gear from his bedroom closet. David followed her, still musing over what she had told him about the case. As the beautiful woman slipped out of her dove gray Lafayette 148 pants suit and her signature Louboutin heels, he suddenly noticed she was standing there in nothing but lace panties and bra.

Looking up at him as he turned away towards the doorway to give her privacy, she put her training gear down on the bed and walked towards him in her bare feet. "I didn't give you the same courtesy when you were in the shower," she said softly. "Look at me David."

Turning reluctantly to face her, he was struck with her ageless beauty. Recently fifty four human years into this re-manifestation, her skin was flawless, tanned and tight over a muscular but slender body. Impossibly straight hair fell down to her waist, gleaming in the muted light from the floor to ceiling windows.

He met her lapis blue eyes. The yellow ring that appeared in darkness for the Elementals was just barely showing in the dim room. He found himself trembling slightly as she stopped inches away. "I know how you feel David," she said even softer.

To his ears, it sounded like she had shouted those words. Blood rushed through his body at her nearness and he felt like his head might explode from the rising pressure. And, that was not the only part of him feeling the influence of her nearness.

She smiled knowingly. "Allistair and I were talking today about things. Not right now, but I think we may have to change a few things between us to help your powers grow."

David couldn't answer her if he wanted to. His tongue felt frozen to the top of his mouth. If he allowed himself to move, he was sure he would pick her up in his arms and rip off the lacy undergarments she wore. He just shook his head in agreement and she turned and walked back to pick up her gear.

She dressed in moments, the gear a practiced routine. Black high performance tights and coolmax long sleeve shirt. Her hair wound quickly into a long twist down her back. Nike Free sneakers slipped onto her bare feet. No human equipment like a flashlight or weapon were needed by the Elemental to see in the dark, or for protection.

Biting the inside of his mouth hard enough to break open the cut from his recent fall off of Barry and Don's balcony, David composed himself and followed her out onto Peruvian, the street behind his apartment.

She turned to him, looking at his mouth in surprise. "Are you bleeding again?" she asked him.

He reached up to wipe a trickle of blood on his sleeve. His gear was identical to hers. The black would hide the blood. "Must have bitten myself," he mumbled in reply.

She nodded and turned away, walking quickly. She headed west towards the Intracoastal Waterway. David followed, curious as to why they were headed in the opposite direction of the crime scene. Dr. Ma broke into a run as they crossed South Lake Drive and took the footpath along the docks northbound.

Considering their attire and rapid pace, David was hoping nobody noticed them enough to alert the Palm Beach Police Department. Two people dressed in black training gear and running at top speed away from the populated area of the island could be considered a high priority response.

Reaching the tiny round about at the east end of the Okeechobee bridge, Ma veered sharply left and in one stride leapt onto the guard rail on the concrete abutment. Continuing her trajectory, she transformed as she vaulted off the railing towards the Intracoastal Waterway.

A massive wingspan rippled out to allow her to glide upward with one powerful beat. Her long black hair and black training gear seamlessly transformed into the shiny scales of her beautiful Elemental dragon.

As David leapt onto the railing behind her, he heard a sharp "Stay," from her in his mind. Balancing on the rail gracefully, he watched her bank around and pick him up in a rush of wings and talons. As gentle as she tried to be, he always winced from the rough power of her grip on him.

"I want to fly in from the West to ensure the path of arrival or departure of whatever left our dead girl on the roof," Ma said in his mind.

"I could have just met you there," David responded, squirming slightly in her uncomfortable grip.

"I know you don't like flying with me David," she laughed in his mind. "I need you to look down while I look up, to check for signs. From up here, (they were about two hundred feet up) we can catch it all en-route."

David grumbled in agreement. His Tiger self did not like being carried along with her in flight at all if it wasn't absolutely necessary. Sometime she did it as payback for him being difficult, but this wasn't one of those times.

Sweeping down over the beach as the two arrived over the crime scene, Ma said, "I am going to drop you in the ocean offshore so I don't have to fly too low. Transform or don't but you may not like the landing in human skin."

Before he could object to her plan, she let go of him and he dropped quickly towards the black, rippling water below. He judged they were about 100 yards offshore. Closing his eyes and letting his human visage peel away in his mind, he felt the physical shift of his transformation to an Elemental Tiger. Over a thousand years of this ability and he still marveled at the transformation.

A loud splash that would have been visible and audible to anyone along the shoreline announced the Tiger's breaking the water surface. It was Summer, and the population of the island was at it's annual low. There was nobody on the roadway, beach, or in the houses adjacent to the area.

Tigers are powerful swimmers. David's eyes took on their Elemental hue of deep lapis blue with a bright yellow ring around the iris as he opened them. His massive muscular body with its thick coat of steel gray fur and black stripes swept towards the shore with purposeful strides. In minutes he was emerging from the water on the sandy beach.

Ma circled above him, sharp raptor like eyes of the same hue as his raking over the scene. Every tiny thing, living or not, was revealed in her detailed vision. Dragons, like birds of prey, could even see things in varying light spectrum. She could now see the traces left behind of the Otherworldly being that had dropped the dead woman on the beach house roof.

David padded over to the beach house on silent paws and did his own search from the ground. His mouth opened, tongue gaping. Raising his chin while wrinkling his nose, he took in the full spectrum of scents around him. Just like any member of the cat family, he used the Jacobson's organ in his mouth to add the rich miasma of scents to the olfactory section of his brain.

Ma landed next to him silently, waiting until he was done circling and climbing around the beach house. He carefully avoided the crime scene tape and any areas of interest to the human police. He couldn't help leaving huge footprints in the soft surfaces as he passed.

"Nothing out of the ordinary from my end," David said as he transformed back to his human guise and walked toward the dragon waiting silently on the beach. Tigers use smell for environmental mapping, his assessment would have been very exact, as he was familiar with the area.

"I expected as much," Ma answered in his head. If she had spoken to him it would have sounded unintelligible to his now human ears. In her dragon form she didn't have the vocal chords to articulate human language.
"What about from above?" he asked.

"There is a clear path from directly above the roof, heading north," she replied. "Whoever left her came just close enough to put her down and leave back along the route they took to get here."

David looked at her. Glittering black skin picking up particles of light from the every surrounding ambient source. Standing as she was with her wings folded against her body, she could appear almost human in the darkness. Long muscular arms ended in talon like fingers and elegant legs ended in a more reptile looking foot with even longer talons, but otherwise her shape was that of a beautiful woman.

Or he was just used to her.

"What?" she teased. It came out as a soft hiss, but he understood her. "You better watch that look mister, I may take you up on it to increase your power."

David laughed. "You were going to tell me what you and Allistair discussed," he reminded her.

"Jeremy saw a Water Sprite the night of the vision," she said to him mentally. "He almost shot it. I am pretty sure it was because he held me in his arms during the vision."

"And he likes you," David growled slightly. A human had to respond intimately to an Elemental for them to meld their energy with them. Apparently, it had allowed a temporary transference. Still, Jeremy seeing an Otherworldly clear enough to want to shoot it was surprising.

"Easy Tiger," Dr. Ma said softly in his head. "One of the things I worry most about in merging our energies to increase your power is exactly that, jealousy."

David stopped, suddenly understanding where she was going with her earlier line of *changing things* between them. She was right, he would be a handful around anyone showing interest in her if they became physically close. He wouldn't be able to help himself. Avo had the same problem she had told him.

He cleared his throat and changed the topic of conversation. "What are you going to do with the trail you see?"

"I am going to follow it tonight," she announced. "You never know how long it will stay in place and I don't want to lose the advantage. Go home and call Allistair to pick you up. Get the small plane ready and fly to New York tonight. I will see you at the apartment in Manhattan."

They kept a beautifully furnished and very secure residence at 834 Fifth Avenue, in the Lenox Hill neighborhood. Allistair had bought it for them in 1930 just before it opened to public sale. The architect, Rosario Candela and his partner Arthur Hamon did quite a lot of business with uber wealthy Otherworldly's like the three famous Elementals.

"May I run home?" David asked, "Or are you going to fly me to the docks and drop me in the water again?"

She didn't answer him as she stepped close enough to touch him. He could feel the intensity of her thoughts as she closed the space between them. It was almost enough make him step back from her. Almost.

She wrapped her long Dragon's arms around him, followed by her massive wings. He felt trapped in her embrace, unable move. In his human guise, he truly wouldn't have had the power to break her embrace of him if he wanted to.

Opening her mouth, he briefly saw the glitter of wickedly sharp teeth. The talons at the end of her fingers bit into his lower back and buttocks causing him to gasp from the sudden pain. Then she lowered her head to his neck and shoulder on one side and sank her teeth into him.

David felt as if a thousand shards of glass imbedded themselves with her bite. Shards that were splintering off and racing through his body, exploding sensation all over his human nervous system. The effect was so powerful, he couldn't speak. His body felt like strong currents of electricity were running through him.

"Relax," she said in his mind. "Enjoy. This is what you wanted, isn't it? Let's see if even a small taste of being together raises your abilities."

He couldn't answer her. All the sensation has coalesced into the strongest sexual response he had ever felt to anything, anyone. He wasn't even sure where it was located. His whole body felt the overwhelming response. He closed his eyes, grateful she was holding him up. Surely he would be kneeling in the sand at her feet if she let go.

"Transform," she said to him in his head. "Bring me the tiger. Your human form is too fragile."

He tried. To do anything. Nothing happened. He couldn't change anything. He couldn't break the the crystalline grip of sensation she had locked him in. He tried again. "I, I can't," he got out. "Let me go."

"Transform!" she said again, releasing her first bite and imbedding her teeth on the other side.

The waves of sensation were different this time. Stronger. He struggled to do as she asked. Nothing.

"Allistair!" she called in her hissing dragon voice. "Can you see us?"

"I can," came the Elemental snake's voice in both their heads. David started, not sure he wanted the Snake watching this strange scene.

"What does the Tiger look like to you?" she asked silently. To David she said, "Feel me David, let go and meld your essence with mine, don't let the sensation hold you suspended in the Earthly plane."

David wasn't sure what she was asking him, but he tried. This was new and unexpected. Allistair's voice came again in his head. "Brighter I think. He looks much brighter."

Ma seemed to be satisfied with this answer and released her hold on David. As expected, he quickly found himself kneeling at her feet. He didn't have the strength to stand. He also felt like he had just had the most exhausting sexual encounter of this or any prior lifetime.

Ma knelt beside him in her Dragon form and softly, with her sandpaper Dragon's tongue, licked the blood from her bites off both his shoulders. The sensations from earlier rose again, unbidden. David groaned softly. He didn't know how much more he could take of this.

"Rest a bit," Ma said to him and rose to her feet. "I will see you in New York. You should be better able to take care of yourself now." A few powerful beats of her wings and she was gone. Straight up she rose and disappeared into the night sky.

As the sand she stirred slapped and stung his skin, David thought, "At least my tiger foot prints will be obscured, along with anything else of evidentiary value. I hope they got it all before we disturbed the crime scene."

The soft susurrus of the waves and the humid salty tang of the beach air surrounded him. He felt like he could barely move. "Allistair?" he called in his mind.

"Yes?" came the chuckling response from the Snake.

"Please come get me," David said softly, closing his eyes.

Chapter Six - Life Lessons

As she flew, Dr. Ma thought seriously about what she had started with David. The case investigation was easy at this point. All she had to do was fly along the route taken by the Otherworldly who had left the dead body.

The path was clearly visible to her. It appeared to be a trail of silvery particles suspended in the air. She flew just above it for perspective, not because she could disturb it. Nothing could disturb it until the energy that made it faded from existence.

When she found the creature who made it, she would be glad to help it fade from existence. For good.

Her thoughts wandered to the last memory she had in her mind of her creator. He was also David's creator. Both she and David were so different and yet fitted exactly for their purpose here on Earth. David's tiger was the Yang to her dragon's Yin. Together they formed the perfect balance.

Just like the ancient depiction of Yin and Yang. The white and the black each formed their own bodies in an endless circle. The infinite tails of each color melding into the other. Each body also held the tiniest dot of the opposite color, if the image was rendered correctly.

Ice crystals were forming on the tips of her wings. She dropped to a lower altitude. The cold didn't bother her and she could simply breathe fire onto her wings to de-ice them, but there was no reason to fly that high. She was busy thinking and had wandered off course.

Dropping below the cloud layer, she turned her thoughts to the last time she had seen him. The Adept who had created her.

The old man, stood alone on the cliff, raw silk robes rippling in an unseen wind around his thin body. The very cliff where she had so recently taken flight.

It was her first flight, one of many, but never one to return to him.
No, never. Ever. As it was supposed to be.

He had done his part. He made her and sent her off to do what was needed. She didn't have to look back physically to see him and hear him in her mind. He was a part of her.

Very softly under his breath, in her memories, she heard him say, "As long as time endures, and sentient beings remain on your Earth, good will prevail."

She knew he was speaking to someone else, not her. Someone unseen, but burned forever in his memories. Kaia, the Elemental mother of Earth, her Adept's great love and David's mother. Ma knew this, but the tiger didn't.

She watched him take a final look in the direction he had last seen her in flight. "Good bye beautiful one," he had said. The morning fog on the mountain, acrid from the decomposing earth, brought her the scents of home. She was sure she would never see it all again.

He seemed to sigh to himself as he turned away from her. She watched him retrace their route slowly back down the mountain path.

Her Dragon's heart ached at the memory. She wished she could ask him what to do about David. She wondered who had been Avo's mother. Was it Kaia? Avo never knew.

"Kaia!" she called to the air around her. "I know you can hear me! Tell me what I should do? I am afraid to destroy your gentle son, trying to make him stronger. I am trying to keep him safe. He is nothing like the first tiger. Give me some guidance."

The frigid air blew over and around her. Silence was all that greeted her as she flew progressively north towards New York. She knew the Earth mother heard her. The problem was, they only answered when they had something to say. Apparently she was on her own.

David knelt there long after she left, gathering his thoughts and letting the sensations in his body fade enough to try and stand. "What the hell just happened?" he thought. Was that how Elementals mated? He wouldn't know, never having done so in his thousand years on Earth.

He was a bit freaked out by the whole thing. It was not at all what he expected. Then, he never expected to be any closer to Ma than he had been for the last millennia. She was a Dragon and already had a Tiger mate for a millennia after their Adept had created them. A power couple created to fight Otherworldly bad guys.

David was version two. The first Tiger had passed from the Earthly plane and he had been drafted to take his place. But that was another story all in itself. Ma and he were infinitely close, but not like that. Not that he hadn't dreamt of being with her since the first time he met her.

She rescued him in his first manifestation at seventeen human years of age. Already a powerful warrior and designated leader of a mountain people of ancient Greek origins, he was freshly undead. Rather, he had died and been restored if you will, to a new self that could transform into an Elemental Tiger.

Freaky stuff for a newbie. Then Ma had swept in and taken him under her wing, literally, and they had been together ever since. He understood he had a job to do with her, saving humans from bad guys and gals they wouldn't have been able to fight off otherwise. But that was about it.

As a seventeen year old, vibrantly healthy male, he had been immediately interested in Ma sexually. That interest had never waned. It also had never been realized. Now what? He wasn't sure what had happened. He had always been madly in love with the dragon.

He couldn't say she seemed to be talking about anything at this moment but a physical connection to increase his abilities. Certainly she didn't seem to be referring to a loving relationship with a lifetime mate.

Physical connections he had, and could have with anyone he wanted through the last thousand years. Just not with her. He wanted something different with her.

He did feel different though. Sharper if that was possible. Clearer. That is how he heard the approach of the familiar smelling human sooner than ever before. Soon enough to strip the gun out of the detective's hand that was pointing at him.

"Police! Put your hands up!" Jeremy Brenner shouted, pointing a wicked looking Sig Sauer 45 cal semi auto directly at his chest. David reacted instantly, way ahead of Brenner's intent. The taller man reached forward and snatched the firearm away, tossing it into the sand in one swift motion.

David then stood there, hands up palm forward in the Universal sign for surrender. "Jeremy!" he said loudly to get the cop's attention. "It's me, David."

Brenner had shifted backwards and withdrawn his department issued Taser stun gun from its holster on the other side of his waist. Letting a projectile fly with a practiced pull of the trigger, Brenner then dropped to one knee to retrieve his backup firearm, a Glock 27 from his ankle.

"I don't know if it's you David, because I am not sure what the hell you are," Brenner answered.

David felt the business end of the Taser dart imbed itself in his skin and reached for the small dart to pull it free. Brenner immediately hit him with a twenty second burst of electricity.

David staggered back from the sudden pain and said "You shot me!"

"Not yet," Brenner said grimly. He now pointed the Glock 27 at David. He had swapped the Taser to his weak hand and held the Glock in his strong one, balanced perfectly along the top of his weak wrist .

David was shocked speechless, but the predator in him was taking over from the pain, fear, and anger at the detective's actions. "No!"

he said to himself. Struggling against the growing urge to transition, he called out to Allistair. Jamil answered him first. The ancient guardian wasn't usually awake without prior notice.

Residing in a scraggly and very old sand pine tree off Flagler Drive, the powerful Guardian protected a ley line that ran through Florida. He had helped Dr. Ma and David many times in the past. "Be still David," the ancient and gravelly voice came to him."The human has a strong image of you and the Dragon investigating and then from your, ah, mating ritual on the beach."

This night could not get any weirder. David went stock still as directed. "How could Jeremy have seen them? Were Dr. Ma's abilities still running rampant in the detective's veins?" he thought. Brenner was standing behind him now, pulling his arms behind his back and handcuffing him while he knelt on the damp beach sand.

The Taser dart was left in place and the muzzle of the firearm was pressed against his neck. He hoped Ma's bite wounds had healed. David didn't want the detective any more freaked out than he was right now.

"I have a surveillance camera set up on the wall," he said pointing with his free hand. "It's not taped because I don't have a warrant but I was monitoring it tonight, hoping for a break in my case." The man's voice was trembling slightly. To his credit though, the detective's hand on the firearm seemed quite steady.

"Jeremy," David began. The detective put a knee on David's back and a hand on the opposite side of the taller man's head while he pressed the muzzle of his gun harder into David's neck. "Please don't shoot me." David wouldn't die as an Elemental. Killing them was much harder than that. He would die as a human if Jeremy took that shot. Some things couldn't be healed in time to survive. Even at an accelerated rate.

"What are you? What was with you and, that thing?"Jeremy was speaking more softly now, his words coming out as tight as an overwound clock mechanism.

"Well," David thought, "this should be an interesting explanation." Aloud he said, "What are you talking about?" Brenner tightened his grip and shoved the gun harder into David's flesh. The knee in David's back slipped lower, pressing painfully on his handcuffed wrists.

"No way man," Brenner shouted. "Don't bullshit me! You, you looked like some sort of giant tiger or something coming out of the water then some dragon like thing landed and I don't even know what happened after you two walked all over my crime scene." The words were rushed, the thoughts scattered.

A familiar voice drifted down to where they were positioned on the beach. "Detective Brenner? Allistair's voice boomed. "Are you there?"

David knew the Elemental Snake could see them as if it were daylight. Brenner called "Over here!"

As Allistair came up to them, David saw a fake look of surprise suffuse the attorney's features. "What is going on!" he boomed.

"I need to call the station, but my cell phone died," Brenner said, not taking an ounce of pressure off of David. "My police radio is in the car, can you call them on your phone for me?"

Allistair immediately took out his cell phone and started dialing. When the call was answered, he leaned forward to hand it to Detective Brenner. The recorded voice that was saying "You have reached the offices of McGowan and McGowan," never got through to Jeremy Brenner. The moment his free hand touched Allistair's he froze in place for the briefest second and then pitched forward, unconscious.

Reflexively pulling the Taser trigger on the way down, he delivered another shot of electricity to David, who dropped to his side grunting in pain until Allistair pulled the weapon from the detective's stiff hand. "I need one of these," he joked. "Looks like I could easily disable you and have my way," he began before David hooked him behind one knee with one foot, and dropped him into the sand next to him.

"Shut up and help me get this mess cleaned up," David said angrily.

"That is a ten thousand dollar suit you just messed up boy," Allistair grumbled. "What are you worried about. When Brenner wakes up, he won't remember anything since, well I gave him a good shot of memory eraser. He should be awake again, let's say, this morning sometime."

David had slipped his cuffed hand over his buttocks and feet to standup and go through the detectives pockets for a key. The dart was pulled out and reset in the Taser. The cuffs were replaced in the detective's case as well as both Glocks retrieved and wiped off before tucking them into their respective holsters.

David picked up the detective like he weighed nothing and carried him to the roadway where his car was parked. Brushing off most of the sand on him, he sat him in the car, his head resting on his hands on top of the steering wheel.

"Hopefully he will think he fell asleep," David said, pushing Allistair towards his black Mercedes parked behind Brenner's car. "Let's go before some enterprising young cop comes by to check on the detective."

They quickly got into Allistair's car and drove south on South Ocean Boulevard. "I assume we are going straight to the airport?" David said wearily.

"Yes," the attorney responded. "I saw and heard everything, so of course I was already preparing things. Glad I kept in touch, the Brenner thing I did *not* expect."

"That makes two of us," David agreed. "It has been a crazy night."

"Tell me all about it," Allistair said smiling lasciviously.

"I should have guessed you would enjoy my misery," David said glumly. "I need to re-manifest at least once where something bad is not happening to me on a daily basis."

"Serves you right for how good looking you come back each time," Allistair grinned.

David just shook his head at him. Then he said, "I hope you have food on the plane. I'm starving."

"Of course," the stocky smaller man replied. "No tempting you to transition and eat the pilot in flight."

"I do not eat meat," David said. "Ugh. Please. Where are we flying into?"

"Teterboro," the attorney answered. "Get us into Manhattan faster. Not that Ma needs us to help her track the Otherworldly."

"Do you know what it is yet?" David asked. He knew Allistair had probably visited the Library to determine who they were hunting for.

"Would you believe Pazuzu?" Allistair said, shaking his head in the negative.

"What?" David said sitting up, his fatigue temporary gone. No wonder Ma had thrown a hail mary pass before she took off. She was really trying to strengthen him. "Hanbi's son? Seriously?"

"Yes," Allistair said grimly. "She is positive it was him that left the woman's body on the beach house roof, but she doesn't believe he killed her. He can be evil, but for the most part, he protects humans from Otherworldly bad guys. Besides, what interest would he have in the murdered woman?"

"What did Berenice and Maia think?" David asked.

Berenice and Maia were the gatekeeper and librarian respectively, of the Library. Berenice II, was the wife of Ptolemy III, 240 BCE. Since she never died (contrary to popular belief), she chose to help the Elementals care for the real Library of Alexandria.

Dr. Ma had never been able to discover exactly where Berenice originated as an Otherworldly being. The pretty woman could even manifest in human guise very convincingly if needed.

Maia worked with them, as immortality can be tedious. She was happy to have something to do with her time. She kept the contents in order and constantly added new materials. Maia was always in Spirit form and didn't manifest in human or any other solid guise on the Earthly plane. Yet, that is.

The two women originated from a time when Pazuzu would have been well known. Their opinion could be valuable.

"Same as Dr. Ma," Allistair said in his clipped and efficient manner. "Not the actual killer. Don't know why he would be involved in moving the body. Seems beneath him actually."

"Agreed," David said thoughtfully. "We should look at how he could become so involved and that may point us in the right direction."

They drove the rest of the way in silence.Except for the grumbling noises from David's stomach. "My god you have a fast metabolism," Allistair complained. "I know you ate at Barry's party." The smaller man turned to David and lifted one eyebrow inquiringly.

"Don't go there," David warned. He expected the man to tease him about everything that went on.He was too tired and hungry to hold his own with the clever snake. It would have to be hashed over later. He kept thinking about Jeremy Brenner slumped over in his unmarked patrol car.

"Maybe we should make an anonymous call to the station to say we thought the cop in the car looked asleep," David said.

"I thought you were his friend," Allistair retorted as he pulled up to the private hanger and got out. "Come on, let's get in the air. If you call on a recorded line and say he is sleeping in his car he will get in trouble."

"I guess you are right," David said, ducking as he entered the small plane. He nodded to the captain and took a seat. There was a bag of his preferred snacks and a large bottle of water in the seat next to him. "Thank you," he said to Allistair as he fell on the food and practically stuffed it down.

Allistair rolled his eyes, smiling as he drained the small glass of sherry the flight steward handed him. "I'll have another right after takeoff," he told the man.

The steward nodded and moved off towards the back of the plane. The plane was soon in the air and heading north towards Manhattan and the next clues to the murder. David's long frame was stretched out between the chair he was sitting in and the two next him. His eyes were closed. It had been an incredibly long day.

Allistair regarded him thoughtfully before clearing his throat. He was on his third sherry. His reptile like metabolism didn't allow for him to become intoxicated per say, but the alcohol made him happy and relaxed. David opened his eyes and looked at him, knowing what would be the next probable topic of conversation.

"So," Allistair said. "You and Dr. Ma finally, eh?"

David groaned audibly. "Really? You are going to go there now?"

The stocky man frowned, staring at him intently. An immaculate three piece suite in steel gray pinstripes, a starched white button down shirt and scarlet silk tie added to the impression of seriousness. His custom Italian leather shoes gleamed in the dim light of the cabin.

"No need to discuss it because you did such an outstanding job your first time with her?" he said. "Remember I saw and heard everything. You looked like a rabbit frozen in the headlights of an oncoming car. Then it ran you over."

David flushed with embarrassment. "I had no idea what was going on, nor what to do," he began hotly. This was a dramatic change for the usually quiet and reticent tiger.

"Ah, she was right!" Allistair said, his face lighting up. "You are definitely changed already. Good job!"

David sat up and lowered the caliber of his voice, almost growling. "I am the only one who doesn't know the particulars of this plan. I feel like an idiot and I don't like it." His upper lip was slightly curled and he looked angry.

Allistair regarded him quietly for a moment before speaking. "Yes, you have a right to be angry. She did not prepare you for it. In her defense, she was going to but something must have happened on the beach that made her leave quickly and want to protect you."

"Protect me? How? I don't understand." David looked away. He seemed to be composing himself. A confrontation between the two powerful Elementals was not the best idea in a small plane in flight. For many reasons.

The Cessna Citation M2 that they were flying in was their go to short distance option. Small but comfortable, it met their needs for brief flights within the Continental USA. They had another, its twin, in Italy for Allistair's use in Europe and Asia.

Their Boeing 787-9 jet was what the three Elementals used for transatlantic travel. It had seen its share of use this year already. Their pilot and co-pilot lived in a luxury apartment in downtown West Palm Beach, close to the airport now that Allistair had relocated his main offices.

The pilot and co-pilot husband and wife, were former IDF, Israeli Defense Force pilots. They had been with the three for over a decade now, and were fiercely loyal and incredibly discreet.

The plane steward was a human and Air Spirit halfbreed like Tam, Dr. Ma's bike shop owner. The man loved his job. He never felt so happy as when they were in flight. Allistair had arranged private living quarters for him at the plane's hangers since he started with them one hundred and forty years prior. Half humans usually had 2-3 time the life expectancy of their human parent.

Allistair had paused, struggling for the best way to explain. Never known for his subtle approach, he decided to go for broke.

"She may literally roast me for discussing this with you, but what the hell," he said. "After Jeremy could see the Water Sprite the other night, she figured you may have been struggling to fully develop your abilities for the last thousand years due to your, ah, lack of physical contact with her. Your balance in power."

David stared at him uncomprehending for a moment and then, like someone turning on a light in a dark room, he caught a glimpse of the other Elemental's thoughts. "Well, f-ck me!" he said.

"Yes," Allistair agreed dryly. "Exactly what she should do."

David turned bright red. He could feel the flush of heat over his face and cheeks. "I don't want her to do that.' he stammered.

"What?" Allistair burst out laughing. "That is all you have ever wanted since I have known you! You have been madly in love with her forever. Not that it wasn't expected. I told her she needed to give up the *mated for life* nonsense and, you know, give you are shot."

"No," David said, softly. "That's not what I meant." The other man leaned forward slightly, one eyebrow raised, waiting for him to go on. "her to just f-ck me I mean, I don't want that. I am in love with her. I want what she and Avo had, not just sex."

"Oh my," Allistair said, raising both eyebrows in surprise. "I don't know *anyone* who would turn her down big guy. You would be a first to give her the *no casual sex* caveat. Say, are you sure you are a **male** tiger?"

David gave him a sideways glance and growled in response. Allistair laughed out loud. "It's a little girly to insist on a relationship instead of just sex."

David frowned. "She said she was worried about my responses around her if we had a relationship."

"True," the other man said. "Avo could be a pain in the ass, all territorial and such. Not that he had any reason to be. She is a one man, well, one Tiger, Dragon. In the event she decides on that one man, or Tiger, whatever. But on to your complete paralysis when she shared her energy with you on the beach. What gives?"

"I, I don't know," David said, rubbing his hands over his face with obvious fatigue. "I felt like I was touching a live electrical wire. Even though I could feel everything, I couldn't move, much less transform."

"It is a unique experience," Allistair agreed. "Nothing can prepare you for it."

"You and Ma?" David said, his face draining of color.

"No, no!" the other man was quick to correct him. "Not that I would turn her down of course. Look, David, a small experiment for you. When we land and get to the apartment I will work with you to see if we can get you over the shock and better able to respond to her."

David looked at him, his brow furrowed. The other man was holding out his hand to the steward for another drink. "Are you sure that alcohol isn't getting to you? Are you offering to have sex with me?"

"Hmph," Allistair said rolling his eyes. "You should be so lucky. No, she told me not to. I am just going to teach you to share energy so it will be easier. We aren't always having sex when we just merge our energies."

David thought about it for a moment and nodded his assent. The quiet motion of the plane soon lulled him into an uneasy rest. His meditative state was anything but regenerative with everything going on in his head from the past eighteen hours.

Chapter Seven - Evil Lives In Manhattan

Dr. Ma landed lightly on the rooftop of the building in Manhattan. "Nice address," she thought. She was on the roof top of 998 Fifth Avenue in the Upper East Side.

Not far from her own place on the same street. She was familiar with the neighborhood. She was *very* familiar with who lived in the building. Pazuzu had been a resident here since construction was completed in 1912 by Jacquie Kennedy's grandfather, James Lee.

The Italian Renaissance style palazzo building, boasted tall glass windows, lighting the seventeen private residences on the twelve floors. One window, a custom, narrow French door styling, was open on the ninth floor. Gauzy curtain fabric billowed out. There was not a breeze. It was also Summer in the city. The heat made it unlikely a luxury apartment wouldn't be closed against the grime and noise, and air conditioned to the hilt.

Except for Pazuzu's digs. He was expecting her.

She landed easily inside the window opening, folding her wings against her body. She did not transform out of her powerful Elemental shape. Who knew what the welcoming committee was going to be like.

"Long flight?" came a familiar voice. It sounded like a storm wind blowing sand against an old wooden door. Her raptor like vision picked him out immediately, standing in the center of the room. He was in his Otherworldly form. Black skin, large feathered wings and a mostly human body, his legs ended in taloned animal feet. On his head was a typically Egyptian headdress. His visage was more demon-like animal than human.

They stared at each other for a long moment and then both swiftly transformed into their respective human guises. Smiling, they walked forward and embraced. "Good to see you again my friend," Ma said.

"Likewise Ma-sama," the demon wind king said, nodding respectfully. "We live so close and never socialize."

Ma laughed and accepted his offer to sit in his richly appointed central living room. "I love this building," she remarked. "We should try harder to get together when we are in New York. It's not as if we have forever to catch up."

They both laughed at this and Pazuzu offered her a glass of wine. "I last spoke to you when you were consulting on that *Exorcist* movie sequel."

"You and David were away when we did the original," he remarked. "Allistair stopped by with a nice bottle of wine and his congratulations on the realism we managed to convey."

"Very real," Ma remarked, her eyes narrowed. "You didn't actually *assist* with any of the special effects, did you?"

"Now Dr. Ma," the demon protested in his rich, sexy baritone. "I am reformed. I *help* humans like you Elementals do."

"Of course," she said, setting down her wine glass untouched. "You know why I am here?"

Pazuzu sighed and drained his glass before setting it down next to hers. "That is a 2013 Caymus 'Special Selection' Cabernet," he pouted. "Your attorney would," he began.

"Drink the whole bottle," she laughed. "I know. Look, my time is a bit pressed. I had to clear a day at my Clinic tomorrow to come here to investigate the murder of the young woman you left on the roof."

"I cannot believe you two work for a living," he said, shaking his head. "Gives us immortals a bad name. She was left on my roof, where you so recently landed, and I merely delivered her home if you must know."

"Who left her on the roof?" Ma inquired, "and what condition was she in then?"

"Dead as a, what do the kids say, doorknob," the demon said excitedly.

"I am pretty sure the kids today no longer say that. You need to get out more. Dead from what?" she prompted. Speaking with demons was never simple. Pazuzu may allege that he was reformed and doing good, but like all demons, they often spoke in riddles to confuse.

The demon stroked his chin, looking puzzled. "That is the million dollar question," he said. "As in, she came to the party offering a million dollars to duplicate my party at their digs. Then she died at some point. I'm sorry she froze on the trip to Palm Beach, but I fly at high altitudes. You know how it is."

Dr. Ma did know how cold the upper altitudes were. That was why she couldn't take the Tiger on this trip by carrying him. He would freeze. She didn't have the same issue with her Elemental reptile blood. Neither did the eternally hot demon. He kept himself from freezing with his boiling blood temperature.

"You are telling me you couldn't tell how she died?" Ma said surprised.

"I know, right?" the Demon said. "Me? The master or dastardly deeds. Uh, formerly the master I mean. Not a mark, nothing."

"Are you sure she was dead?" Ma asked.

Pazuzu started and looked at her in complete surprise. "What are you implying? I didn't kill her!"

"I'm not saying you did," Ma said soothingly. "I'm just asking if you knew for sure she was dead. A Spirit Wind came to me about her death. I saw you and I saw her, but not how she died. It was as if she didn't know she was dead."

"Came to you in Florida?" Pazuzu asked in clarification. He looked slightly paler for a moment. "Did I kill her by freezing her to death flying her down? Oh crap, I am supposed to be doing good now. Really, there was no sign of life."

"What was the sign of death?" Ma asked. Only an Otherworldly could answer this properly. Human's look different to Otherworldly eyes when they are dead. Sort of see through, and almost empty, like a shell of their former selves.

Pazuzu paused. "I may have been a bit drunk from a small party we had on the rooftop," he looked at her sheepishly. "I woke up and everyone was gone but me and the dead girl."

Ma rolled her eyes and paused a moment to gather her thoughts. "So you threw one of your drunken orgies on the roof and, wait, you don't sleep, how did you wake up?"

The Demon paused. " I must have passed out. I have never done that before." He frowned. "You can't drug something like me, can you?"

"Who was at the party Zu?" she said, using his nickname.

"Seriously?" he asked her incredulously. "Who wasn't would be more like it. It was one of *my* parties after all!"

"Take me up to the rooftop and show me the layout. Who else in the building goes up there?" she said.

"I own it," he said dryly. Nobody goes there without my permission. Anyone that wants to come back I mean."

"Good to know," she remarked.

"Oh, not you Ma-sama, of course," he corrected himself. Let me show you the setup."

They took a private elevator from the hallway that led to the roof. The entire ninth floor was Pazuzu's apartment. This was evidently the only access to the roof. From the plethora of Otherworldly guards in the hallway limiting egress and ingress, Ma assumed the killer and the victim would have been invited guests.

You could attend one of the famous Demon's parties by direct invitation of an Otherworldly if you were human, but that was the only way.

The rooftop was laid out like an outdoor garden around the elevator access. Dr. Ma had landed on the roof behind the building maintenance structures and hadn't seen this side.

Ma stopped suddenly, Pazuzu almost running into her. "What's wrong?" he said.

"Nothing," she answered. "I just want to see it from a wide perspective. Have you had another party since that night here?"

"No," he shook his head in the negative. "I figured I would wait a bit. I haven't had a dead human show up, ever, in one of my parties."

"Do you think this is about you?" Ma asked curiously.

"I don't know," he replied. "Why would she be left here if it wasn't?"

"Good point," Ma thought, but refrained from saying anything. She walked forward and swept her raptor like gaze left and right, looking under and around all the trace Otherworldly presence trails for something human.

Looking for the sign of Otherworldly visitation in the human population was easy. One glittering path would wind wherever they went. Looking among the hundreds of overlapping paths in a recent Otherworldly party for the human trail was harder.

It would be there if she was diligent about finding it. Among the glitter would be a dark line absent of the sparkling paths of Others like her. Picture someone running a pencil eraser through a glitter filled Holiday scene on a greeting card. The line devoid of sparkles was the human one.

In this case the two lines devoid of sparkles were the two humans. Only two in a sea of Otherworldly trails. "Who were the two humans at the party?" Ma asked.

"Who were the what?" Pazuzu looked at her slightly confused. "You expect me to remember who was here? That is what I have human security for. We can review the video feed in the security office if you wish."

"I wish," she confirmed.

They took the elevator back to the demon's floor and walked to the opposite end of the hallway from his front entrance door. The wall shimmered and disappeared as they walked towards what looked like a tall window looking out onto Fifth Avenue.

"Nice setup," Dr. Ma commented as they simply walked into Pazuzu's security office. It encompassed the entire end of the hallway on his floor. Computer screens paneled the room with feeds of every aspect of the building, hallways and rooms.

She could easily tell that every security person in the room was human. None had been in the hallway. Interesting. The human security in the room couldn't tell the difference between humans and Otherworldly guests and occupants. No conflict.

Pazuzu quickly gave the date of the party and the time he wanted to view to one of the security personnel. Almost immediately the wall screen the man controlled began showing the feed they requested.

The two humans were easily identified by Dr. Ma and Pazuzu. The Demon pointed to them and asked the man controlling the video feed to track backwards to the time they showed up on surveillance. Seconds later he showed them entering the building together.

During the party, nothing unusual happened to either human except that the female whose dead body was found in Palm Beach seemed to disappear from the party about an hour before it broke up.

"I have a time schedule," Pazuzu explained. "In at a certain time and out at a certain time. I need my beauty sleep."

"It looks like you are already getting some of that sleep," Ma commented, pointing at the Demon stretched out in a chaise on the rooftop. He seemed to be sleeping.

"Pan the rooftop for the hour before and after the end of the party," Pazuzu told the man. Several more screens around them sprang to life as his request was granted.

"There she is," Ma pointed at the woman's body near the point Ma herself had landed this evening. It was on the opposite side of the rooftop from the party.

Pazuzu frowned but didn't comment. A figure dressed in black like a B movie ninja dragged the dead woman's body into sight and left it next to Pazuzu's chaise.

"Zoom in on that," the demon said on a menacing voice. The man at the controls shivered as if he was hit by a blast of cold. The figure was covered head to toe in black. Except the eyes. They were covered by a large pair of sunglasses. It was well after midnight. There was no sun.

"Have whomever was on that camera come to my private office in one hour," the Demon said in a deadly voice. Dr. Ma noticed that the room had gone deathly still. Even the humming of the electronics seemed muted.

"Yes sir," the man answered, visibly shaking. "It was him," Ma thought. He was justifiably terrified. No security alert had been given with an obvious breach by the black garbed person dragging the woman's body.

"You should run for your life," she thought, shielding her thoughts from Pazuzu. "He will get the information he needs and you will never be seen again." She didn't bother to let the man hear her thoughts. He was never going to leave the building now anyway. The Otherworldly guards outside the room had already picked up on the conversation.

She walked back to the demon's main living quarters with him. He was visibly fuming. When they were out of reach of human ears, she said quietly, "We all saw it tonight because it was recorded, but your security man looked like he was seeing it for the first time."

"I know," Pazuzu sighed. "I will pick through his brain and see if I can determine what obscured the event from him before killing him."

"Pazuzu!" Dr. Ma rebuked him. "I thought you had changed. If it wasn't his fault, why kill him?"

"Reputation!" he replied. "Street cred and all. I can't let this go unpunished. They will think I am weak."

"You can't punish him for something he couldn't have prevented," she replied.

"You are getting soft, Dragon," he grumbled. "Alright. I have a small group of, ah, underground employees in the Balkins I can add him to. He has no family so he shouldn't be missed. Much."

"Are you taking him yourself?" she asked him pointedly.

"Yes, yes," he assured her grudgingly. "Don't get all worked up about it. I will let you know if he gives me any useful information. Are you in Town overnight?"

"Yes," she said. "David and Allistair should be arriving at the apartment soon."

"Breakfast at your place tomorrow about 7:00 AM?" the demon asked, eyes glittering.

Dr. Ma laughed. "David and I will be up and back from our run, but Allistair should be pretty pissed off to be ready that early. Deal."

The Demon smiled. "Meanwhile, the other human is my social secretary. Since he brought the dead girl, I will send him to your place tonight. You do a much nicer job of sifting through a human mind without laying a trail of destruction. I would like him whole. He does a good job."

"Thank you Pazuzu," Ma said.

"My pleasure Ma-sama," he said with a slight bow. The Dragon was a powerful being. He had been on her bad side in the past. He preferred not to go there again. "See you in the morning."

Ma smiled. Walking back to the open window she had come in, she leapt off the ledge, transforming seamlessly into her Dragon. She took another once over of the roof, noting nothing new, and headed for her Manhattan digs. "Either you are involved and lying to me demon," she said softly to herself, "or you have a viper in the nest."

The evening was beautiful. Her vision brought her the full miasma of activity on the streets. Living in Palm Beach now, she was always surprised when they visited New York City. The whole placed lived and breathed twenty four seven. It was tiring after a few days.

She landed on the open window sill. Slipping into her human guise, stepped easily into her bedroom at 834 Fifth Avenue. Mort must have arrived shortly after she told him of their last minute travel plans. There was a fire crackling merrily behind a modern glass and bronze grate and she could see the steam from the jacuzzi tub coming from the attached bathroom.

"Good evening Ma-sama," Mort greeted her, materializing from the waist up. "The gentlemen have just arrived."

"Thank you Mort," she said sighing. It had been a long and complicated day. The jacuzzi tub looked inviting. "Tell them we will meet in the dining room in half an hour. We are expecting company. A young man employed by Pazuzu."

Mort wrinkled his nose at the demon's name. "Human?" he inquired.

"Hence the description young *man*," she said. "I am sure he doesn't live with the demon or I would have seen him tonight. Don't go lightning incense everywhere. I know you don't appreciate certain demonic, ah, fragrances." "Hmph," Mort answered. "He will be joining you for dinner if he arrives before you finish?"

"Yes," she said. "If not, we will be meeting in the library afterwards."

Not *THE* Library mind you. That library was easily accessible from her Florida home. This was just a charming room full of books, leather seating and low lighting. True, behind a wall panel was an area to access the dimension where she and Allistair kept the true Library of Alexandria. It just took so much time to get there with all the warding and rigamarole to get in.

The design was to keep anyone else out really, not to just inconvenience her and Allistair from entering.

She had dropped her clothing en-route to the tub, Mort would take care of it before she walked back to dress for dinner. The Djinn was amazingly efficient. The hot and fragrant water felt amazing as she sunk in it up to her shoulders. Lavender, sage, lemon and sea salt were her personal favorites. The jets pounded her stiff and tired human body.

She slipped her head under the water for a moment to wet her hair, so she missed David's catlike entrance to her private sanctum. He was setting down her small toiletry case on the counter when she came up from the water. He spun around so fast he didn't touch the ground until he landed in a crouch.

"Oh my god, that was great!" Ma said laughing so hard tears were coming out of her eyes. "You are so fast when startled. If you were in Elemental form I swear your tail would have the hair standing on end."

David stood up fast from his crouch when he realized it was her and not an intruder. He politely looked away from her naked body and edged backwards towards the bathroom opening. "I, I'm sorry, Mort didn't tell me you were here yet. He left your case downstairs," he said pointing to the small Vuitton on the vanity counter.

He looked so embarrassed she felt sorry for him. Almost. David was so genuine in everything he did he was a perfect target to tease. "Really?" she said standing up and reaching for her towel as she stepped onto the slatted bamboo flooring. The bathroom was designed with a open joint flooring and radiant heated ceramic panels underneath for health and comfort.

She stepped into his exit path and he had to turn towards her to avoid backing into her. Passing her submerged in the tub was a sign of how distracted he really was. It would have been hard to feel her energy under water but there were a dozen other things he could have noticed. Such as the trail of her clothes in the other room.

"I will see you downstairs," he said, trying to get her to let him by without meeting her gaze.

"David," she said, reaching out and lifting this chin so his eyes would meet hers. "Relax. We are going to talk everything out and go step by step from here out. I am sorry I took you completely by surprise on the beach. I just wanted to make you a bit safer. I forgot it would be a shock to you."

He looked at her, quietly studying her face. Now it was her turn to feel uncomfortable. David was always so calm and sure of his path. Life, death, and joy all seemed to rank equally for him. Unless someone interfered with his almost childlike progress around issues. Someone being otherwise manipulative or not entirely truthful. Or insensitive.

"That is just it," he said softly. "I don't want to go step by step and increase my Elemental abilities by, by, whatever that is we did before you left."

She frowned slightly. "What do you mean you don't want that? It can be overwhelming for sure, but..."

He interrupted her. "Not the act, not what I felt when you bit me, although it ranks right up there under craziest sex act ever. I don't want anything between us to be like that. I love you and that has nothing to do with accomplishing a goal of greater powers."

She was at a loss for words. She expected some resistance from him when he realized it was more about the act than the relationship, but she hadn't expected an outright refusal. "I don't understand. Are you saying no to sex with me unless there is a romantic relationship?"

Yes," he said without hesitation. "That's it in a nutshell. I have waited for you my whole existence. If we are not meant to be together then ok. I'm just not interested in the 'R'-rated version of us. I want something else. I want you."

Staring at him for several moments, she realized she had nothing to say to him. She hadn't prepared for this. Not saying what he wanted was going to be painful for both of them. After the tug of war inside her settled down, she merely said, "Okay."

He turned to leave, silent again on his catlike feet. She was sure she could hear the almost audible rip as his gentle Tiger's heart tore in half. Her own reptilian heart, usually cool and detached, felt tight and painful. "This was going to be interesting," she thought unhappily.

Chapter Eight - The Confession

The three Elementals sat down to an elegant dinner setting with several courses. There were paired wines for Allistair. Dr. Ma, oddly out of character, joined him for a glass of Cabernet with her sautéed mushrooms and rice. She wondered again how Mort managed to provide such fare with ease.

It was well after midnight, but none of them actually slept. Rest for their human bodies was all they ever needed besides food and general health maintenance. They were a little lacking in the rest area today, but that small amount wouldn't negatively effect them.

Allistair had been stealing glances back and forth between Dr. Ma and David as they ate in relative silence. She had given him a disapproving look several times, to no avail. She knew he was privy to what had been said between them in the bathroom earlier.

Unless one of the three Elementals guarded their actions or thoughts, both were available to see and hear by the others. In the tightly warded apartment no Otherworldly's could hear them but if they were in public they could be heard easily without precautions.

Mort broke the silence by announcing that their visitor had arrived. Since they were mostly done with their meal, Dr. Ma asked if he would set up dessert and after dinner drinks and coffee in the library. Nodding, the Djinn disappeared to do her bidding.

The human visitor was most likely sitting in the sound proofed entryway on one of the Barcelona chairs placed just for that purpose.

Designed by Mies van der Rohe for the German Pavilion at the 1929 Barcelona Exposition, the black leather and welded stainless steel frames were stylish yet deceptively relaxing. They were some of her favorite pieces in the apartment.

Once the three Elementals were seated in the library, Mort brought the nervous looking young man in to meet them. David stood first, offering his hand. "Thank you for coming, I'm David and this is Dr. Ma and Allistair McGowan," he said turning to include the other two.

"I'm Scott," the slightly disheveled man replied. It was after midnight. He had most likely been roused from sleep and sent to meet with them asap. Or get fired. Normally Scott appeared like a young man who would be meticulous in his appearance.

"Please have a seat Scott," Dr. Ma said pointing to the club chair across from her. The firelight in this room would now play over the young man's features as he faced the crackling blaze behind an etched glass and iron screen. It was not chilly outside. It was chilly inside to keep the Snake happy.

Dr. Ma liked to light the fireplaces when she came to Manhattan. Even in the dead of Summer, as they were now. Scott seemed perplexed by this habit. Pazuzu wouldn't be fond of bright fireplace blazes, even in the Winter. Too similar to the fires of hell sort of scene for the thoroughly modern demon.

All three Elementals regarded the young man sitting with them intently. He shifted nervously under their steady gaze. When Mort entered the room pushing a small cart with desserts, coffee and after dinner drinks, Scott almost jumped out of his chair.

Allistair raised his eyebrows and accepted a brandy laced coffee and chocolate truffle from the Djinn. "Join us?" he inquired of the nervous human.

"No, um, yes please," Scott responded. His hands shook slightly as he accepted the alcohol infused coffee and the chocolate.

"There is nothing to be nervous about Scott," David said in his sensual predator voice. He used this to temporarily immobilize humans. Scott became still, pausing with his truffle halfway to his mouth.

"I cannot believe that cheesy prey/predator voice thing really works," Allistair snapped. He was planning on his own hypnotic stare doing the trick.

"Oh stop it you two," Dr. Ma said standing up. "Scott," she said in a commanding voice, "look at me."

Scott reluctantly took his gaze from David's face and turned slightly towards her. The truffle made it the rest of the way into his mouth. He swallowed more than chewed, and took a sip of coffee.

"We need to know about a young lady who you took to Pazuzu's rooftop party," she said walking a few steps closer to him. She didn't bother with the demon's pseudonym, Mr.

Jones, as the young man must know him well to be his social secretary. It amazed her that some humans didn't mind working in close proximity with Otherworldly beings.

She quickly transformed into her beautiful dragon in front of him. Scott choked and dribbled a blob of coffee and chocolate down his chin. He wiped it away fiercely with his napkin. "Oh god, you are one of them. I thought you might be."

He looked over at David and Allistair, but they didn't transform nor engage him. They just watched him quietly. Looking back at Dr. Ma he said, "Brigette Cohen is who you are talking about, right? The woman found dead in Palm Beach? I brought her to the party but I left early. Ask my wife. Those parties go on all night sometimes."

Dr. Ma listened to his rush of words and nodding, returned to her human guise. "Why did you bring her to the party Scott?"

Curly brown hair spilled over his forehead, just touching the top of a very current pair of Tom Ford black frame glasses. The geek look was in fashion. Scott was not a geek. He was more a wannabe social maven. J Crew casual was his look with an emphasis on too much rumple. He pushed at a lock of his hair. Some sort of nervous tic.

"She and her husband, you know, Barry Cohen the financier, wanted to throw a party like my boss and she wanted a first hand experience. Pazuzu doesn't care, as long as he gets something from it. She said they would invite him and she brought a wad of cash with her. I don't know how she died. Really." He looked at Dr. Ma genuinely confused.

"I believe you," she said in her monotone voice. "I just need to know what you saw that night."

"I, I don't remember much," he began.

"No," she said. "Like this." She got up and crossed to where he sat. Smiling, she bent over and looked him directly in the eyes and placed her hand on his cheek. It would have seemed endearing, except for the sudden stiffening of his body. A slight gasp escaped his lips.

"That smarts," Allistair commented. "Feels like she is slipping a cold needle in your head and twisting it when she is in a hurry."

David nodded in agreement. When Ma had first trained him, after his initial re-manifestation, he had been on the receiving end of her mental rummaging. It was gentler when she just siphoned off memories and thoughts with her silver thread technique. She had done this at their last murder case.

"Problem is," he said to Allistair, "we don't have enough time. She also knows what she is looking for. The other technique is more a discovery mission, sorting and looking."

"I assume I will have to modify his memories when she is done," the meticulously dressed man sighed. "You two will likely be off to roam the city when she finds her information out."

David cocked his head and raised his eyebrows. "So, you can invite your new boy toy up for a nightcap?" He was referring to Allistair's new companion from the building. "We work and you play?"

"I am not good at, nor interested in, all that investigating, my dear Tiger," he said dryly. "Don't begrudge me a little fun. You two are overworking me these days with all this traveling and excitement."

David laughed. "I am only teasing you," he said. "He seems nice, Thomas is it?"

"Yes," the other man smiled slyly. "Actually he has tickets to a show I want to see. It was very convenient that we arrived tonight. I may not be back until you two are ready to fly out. That should give you both a chance to negotiate your issues without me."

David flushed slightly. "I think you know that is not likely to happen."

Allistair shook his head negatively. He reached out a meaty hand and placed it on David's shoulder. "Let it unfold," he said with uncharacteristic seriousness. "I have known her twice as long as you have been alive, or been immortal that is. You are thinking about this all wrong. Just go with the flow."

David didn't respond. Allistair knew his thoughts. He didn't have to elucidate. He could see Ma withdrawing from her inspection of Scott's mind. Almost show time. He started to stand up, but the attorney wasn't finished.

"I don't know an Otherworldly being, including Avo if he could return, that wouldn't take your place," Allistair said quietly. "She has offered you a unique opportunity, whether you like her terms or not."

"Not," David said somewhat shortly, brushing his friend's hand away.

Allistair rolled his eyes. "Idiot" he said under his breath.

"I heard that," the Tiger sent back silently.

"David?" Ma said, fully back in the present and turning to him. "Ready to go? We have an Otherworldly visit to make." She turned to Allistair and indicated Scott, slumped in his chair, unresponsive. "Memory alteration please. Deliver him to his apartment on your way out with, Thomas is it? I hear *"Cinderella"* is quite good."

"Of course," the attorney agreed. "How does she do that?" he thought. Her telepathic skills were legendary.

"I will need you here in the morning for breakfast with Pazuzu," Ma added as she and David headed for the open window. "Sorry."

Allistair grumbled, but he would be there. She wasn't asking his opinion. He took Scott's hands in his and started to backtrack in time to when he arrived at their apartment. Everything after that would be his creation. Permanently.

Dr. Ma transformed and grabbed David as she jumped out the window. He felt the usual stomach dropping anxiety of a sudden take off. "I assume there will be a fight?"

"It is always possible," she responded in his head. "It depends on how loyal he choses to be to the human who paid him. Or his current level of stupidity."

"Who are we talking about?" David responded silently.

"Harry Kellar." she responded.

"The magician?" he said, somewhat surprised. Kellar was a famous magician in New York in the late 1800's. Any Otherworldly being knew he had not died in 1922. Leaving the USA for 80 years, he returned as his own great grandson and was quietly living in Manhattan, at the Plaza Hotel. Allistair handled his affairs as he did for all of them.

"Yes," she said, but then fell silent. He knew she would explain everything eventually. If she left her mind open to him, he could hear her strategizing. But she didn't. He really hated being locked out, a frequent habit of hers. It was that intimacy she refused share with him that caused him the greatest frustration.

Landing on the sidewalk along Fifth Avenue, they entered the Edwardian Room from the street side. There was a little known passage behind the coatcheck area that allowed access through the floors along the exterior walls. There were several such routes in the nineteen story building that didn't appear on any floor plans or architectural drawings.

They passed quickly upward and slipped out of a hidden wall panel on Kellar's floor. He had purchased the suite for his private use in the early 1900's. Despite renovations, his privacy had been maintained. The man himself answered the door when they knocked.

"I was expecting you," he said, glancing behind them and waving them inside. "Please don't dawdle out there, someone could see you."

They brushed past him in the tight front vestibule and heard him lock the door behind them. "Before you even try," Ma said impatiently, "you cannot change matter to effect us. We are Elementals."

The older man walked past them into the center of his living room and stared hard before offering them a seat with a wave of his hand. The air around him rippled, then settled back to normal. He tried again, waving his hand. Nothing.

"Well I had to try," he said, flustered. "Glad to make your acquaintance. Elementals you say? I haven't met one before."

"I am sure of that," David said, looking at the man curiously. There was actually no furniture in the living area. It was a carefully crafted illusion. He knew little enough about them to think they couldn't see past it.

Kellar waved his hand again at the imaginary furniture. There was a hole in the floor that they could tell led to an alternate location. David looked at Dr. Ma and shrugged. She nodded in agreement.

Two steps forward took them level with the immortal magician. Each grabbing an arm, they propelled the man towards the hole and jumped in. "Nooo!" he screamed as they fell together.

The stench of the demon came to them as they descended. "I am going to agree with the last comment you made," David said. "*Nooo* was probably a better idea."

Dr. Ma chuckled and transformed as they neared what appeared to be the floor of a cavern. "I'm up," she said with a strong downbeat of her wings, carrying the magician with her. "Your turn!" she called to David.

David followed suit, landing in full transformation to his Elemental tiger. Ma's Elemental Dragon, swooped in a tight circle above him. The magician had a soft landing on the Tiger as the Dragon dropped him. They didn't want to kill him after all. They needed information.

The older man lay on the floor of the cavern, mouth gaping at the two beings that came with him down the demon hole. "What, what?" was all he could get out.

"Elementals is what," came a booming voice all around them. A large figure emerged from the dark perimeter of the chamber. The Lamassu had the head of a man, body of an ox and wings of a bird. He bowed his head respectfully to Dr. Ma and David. "Great Ones," he said. "Your visit is unexpected. What has the magician done now?"

Dr. Ma landed and transformed to her human guise to facilitate speaking with Kellar and the Lamassu. "I am surprised to see you old one," she addressed the large figure from ancient Assyria. "The stench of demon came from the entrance to your, ah, residence, or we would have made a more respectful arrival."

The man/beast laughed, a booming sound in the confined space. "All for show I'm afraid. A little concoction to mask the magician's true guest. Pretty good if you two thought that was what you smelled!"

David had not transformed back to his human form. He stood quietly poised behind Dr. Ma, his luminous gaze encompassing the entire subterranean cavern. In case there was another surprise. It was not an alternate dimension or location they had jumped into. It was simply a spelled rock cavern.

"Everything alright there tiger?" the Lamassu inquired. David bared his teeth and growled in response. The man/beast took a half step back and bowed his head again. "No reason to get huffy. There is no threat here."

"So you are the origin of the magician Kellar's immortality?" Ma asked.

"Yes," the man/beast agreed. "I should have picked better. He glowered at Kellar. "What have you done to bring two Elemental beings to my chamber?"

The magician scrambled to his feet and looked around at the strange trio. "I simply did a little 'trick' for a client at a party. I don't know why everyone is so worked up."

"Was your trick killing a young woman that attended the party?" Ma asked.

"What? NO!" he said. David's predator hearing caught the immediate increase in the man's heart rate. It seemed loud enough to echo off the walls.

"You killed a woman?" the Lamassu roared. Now the walls were really echoing with sound. The human male fell to his knees, his hands over his ears, moaning.

"No! I was paid to break off the horn of one of the statues on the patio and stir her drink with it. I added a little of my famous sleeping powder for effect. Fell flat though. Nobody even noticed when she passed out. Then ah, I, ah, dragged her to the other side of the roof so she could sleep it off."

"Which statue?" Ma asked.

"The little demon with the blue crystal horns," he answered. "On the mantel?"

"Chalcanthite," she said grimly. "Did you have gloves on?"

"Always," the man sniffed. "Leave no evidence I was there is my motto."

"Lucky you didn't die as well," she said, frowning deeply. "What was in your sleeping powder?" Ma asked, suddenly grabbing him by the shirt front.

"Valerian and chamomile. Perhaps a pinch of aconite." he replied, shaking with fear.

"Idiot!" the man/beast roared. "Did he kill her?" he asked Dr. Ma.

"Yes and no," she replied. She nodded to David and he transformed to his human guise. "He paralyzed her respiratory system and Pazuzu thought she was dead.He flew her home to Palm Beach. She froze to death on the trip."

"Pazuzu?" the man/beast asked. "I haven't seen him in a long time."

"We will see him in a few hours," Ma said. " I will give him your regards."

She turned to the magician. "We know how the non humans were involved in this. Who paid you initially?"

"Her husband," the frightened man croaked. "He wanted her taught a lesson about messing with occult types like Pazuzu."

"She would have died from what you did even if the demon hadn't frozen her to death by accident." She turned to the Lamassu. "I cannot turn Kellar in to the authorities for murder. You will have to deal with him."

"Gladly," the man/beast said, turning his attention to the cowering magician.

Ma transformed and jumped a few feet in the air, unfolding her powerful wingspan to get loft. "Ready?" she asked David.

He reached up and grabbed her waist in answer. It was a short flight back up to Kellar's now very empty looking apartment. The illusion was gone with the illusionist. They had heard his scream of terror cut off before they cleared the cavern's roof.

Transforming back to her human guise, Ma led the way out of the apartment and back down to the street. "Let's walk home," she said to David.

Chapter Nine - A Family Affair

The next morning at breakfast, Dr. Ma and David updated Allistair and Pazuzu on everything that had taken place with the now dead immortal magician and the Lamassu.

"I will send a 'representative' of mine to the Lamassu's ah, *residence*, to see if I can assist him in locating another human contact," Allistair said.

"Make sure the apartment is Trusted to Kellar's surviving relatives so we don't have this issue in the future," Dr. Ma sighed. "Then of course, pick the relative and make them appear as legit as possible. Those Assyrian protection beasts are powerful. We don't want his influence misused again."

"Agreed," Pazuzu said, putting away another chocolate croissant. "I will visit him tonight and catch up. Maybe set him up on a modern form of communication with me in the city. What type of network is he running down there?"

"None," David laughed. "He is truly old school. Just the magician to keep him in contact with the world above."

"OMG," the demon said, swallowing the last bite of croissant with a slurp of coffee. "Maybe I am biting off more that I can chew. What is wrong with keeping in touch with the outside world huh? I get the cave, I mean, he can't transform to a human and all, but no Internet?"

Dr. Ma tapped on her glass with her breakfast spoon to get their attention. "Gentlemen," she said. "My goal is to give our dear friend, Detective Brenner, enough evidence to arrest and prosecute the dead woman's husband. Ideas?"

"My surveillance shows the crime occurring," Pazuzu offered. "My social secretary can place her there and I look innocent, asleep on the chair." He smiled charmingly. "Everything after that was, um, deleted."

"How about a written communication from Kellar to Barry Cohen?" Allistair offered.

"What written communication?" David asked.

"The one I wrote," Allistair answered. "Kellar's girlfriend may have in her possession a certain letter, for safe keeping, in the event my client disappears suspiciously."

"Kellar had a girlfriend?" Pazuzu asked in surprise.

"Great," Dr. Ma said to Allistair. She ignored Pazuzu's comment. We can't use Kellar, lets make it his grandson and Trust the apartment to a charity so we can keep the Lamassu hidden."

"I wish we could catch the bad guys honestly," David said. "How about an undercover sting with the letter Allistair writes, and the cops to see if Cohen may confess?"

"I like that," Dr. Ma said. "We can meet with Jeremy when we get back and explain Allistair's position as Kellar's grandson's attorney. The girlfriend can be given Jeremy's contact information to deliver the letter to him. Let's suggest they try the confession route if our detective doesn't come up with it himself."

"When are we leaving?" David asked. "Winnie said we have a few patients late this afternoon and one of us at least needs to teach the advanced class this evening at the dojo."

"Anytime," Allistair said, wiping the last crumbs of breakfast from his mouth and standing up. "Paz, good to see you. Don't be a stranger. I will let you know when I am in Town again. Dr. Ma and David don't come here as frequently."

The Demon stood up, snatching the last croissant and stuffing it into his pocket with one of their fine linen napkins wrapped around it. "For the walk home," he said sheepishly.

"Mort will skin you if you don't return his napkin," David laughed.

"Will do, will do," the Demon agreed quickly. "That is one snippy Djinn you have there. Known him for ages really."

They all walked to the private elevator and went down to the lobby. Promising to get together soon, the Elementals got in to their waiting SUV and Pazuzu strolled off in the direction of his own apartment building.

It was a sunny Summer day in Manhattan. Smells, sounds and sunlight limited to the height of the buildings around them set the happy and active scene. The events of last night were lost on the passers by. Nobody would miss the immortal magician they didn't even know was still alive.

Nobody would care that an ancient storm entity in the body of a man/ox/bird dwelt beneath one of Manhattan's priciest and most exclusive residential apartments buildings.

Even less would notice the just as ancient and formerly evil demon strolling along the street, stuffing the last bites of a chocolate croissant in his mouth.

They arrived back at the private airport in New Jersey in record time. As promised, the jet was ready and waiting. A short and uneventful flight deposited them back in Palm Beach County, Florida.

Dr. Ma called Detective Brenner as they got into the waiting Towncar. "Jeremy," she said when he answered. "David, Allistair and I just landed. We went to Manhattan overnight and I think we have the break in the murder case you have been looking for."

She was quiet for a moment, listening as he spoke on the other end. "Yes, the Brigette Cohen case. You will never guess who killed her. Can you meet us at my house in about half an hour?"

She hung up and said, "He will be there in about 40 minutes. David, do you want us to drop you at the Clinic first or talk with Brenner?"

"Drop me at the clinic so I can get things going there," David answered. "You don't need me to talk to Jeremy. I will order from Joy's for lunch, do you want something for later?"

"No food for me thank you," Dr. Ma replied. "Allistair and I will grab something at the house and make sure Jeremy eats. He seems to be thinner these days."

"Gracie," David smiled. "He is trying to impress her with his workout ethic.

Dr. Ma smiled back. "A good match. She will keep him on his toes for sure."

Allistair looked at them interestedly. "What am I missing? Our intrepid detective is interested in a new woman?"

"One of our martial arts students, younger than him but very mature," Dr. Ma said in explanation. "Her name is Gracie."

"Anything is better than Circe's daughter," Allistair said off handedly.

David was just getting out of the car in front of the Clinic. "What?" he said, bending his 6'5" frame back down to stick his head in the car.

Allistair suddenly realized he had let the cat out of the bag. Dr. Ma made a hissing sound at him."Ah well," he said, "He was going to find out eventually."

David slipped back into the Town car. The driver had the engine idling as he waited in the roadside parking slots in front of their business in West Palm Beach. "Spill," David said, his handsome tanned face suddenly paler.

"David," Ma began, then stopped. His eyes were hard when he looked at her. He hated her keeping things from him. "When you were attacked at Barry's party, I wanted to tell you that Karen was Circe's daughter and you needed to be careful, but the opportunity didn't come up."

"Bullshit," David said angrily. "That is what the beach thing was all about. You knew she was a danger and you were trying to make me stronger."

"Guilty," Ma said, her gaze equally hard. "I won't apologize for trying to protect you. Besides, we don't know what Karen knows. In fact. I think she may not have realized she could do what she did to you when she threw the vase at you."

"I just found out more myself," Allistair added, trying to explain further. "I did a bit of research in the library and was able to confirm everything. Karen is Joseph McCarthy and Circe's daughter. Ann adopted her knowing she was the child of her rival for Joseph's affections."

David just stared at them. Finally, shaking his head, he got out of the car and walked away towards the front entrance of the Clinic.

"That went well," Allistair said.

"Totally," Ma said, closing her eyes and resting her head on the back of the seat. She tapped on the window and the driver pulled out into traffic, heading for her residence off Flagler Drive.

Winnie looked up as David walked through the front door of the Clinic. "Welcome back," she said.

David mumbled something unintelligible and kept walking towards the back. She knew where he was headed when she heard the back door chime as he opened it.

"Thank you Winnie," she said to herself. "So good to see you as well. Thanks for taking such good care of things while we were gone." She rolled her eyes at her own sarcasm and picked up the phone to order them both lunch from Joy's. She knew he would be hungry soon.

David entered the cool darkness of the attached martial arts school and started peeling off his clothing. Reaching the private office he shared with Dr. Ma, he dropped everything on the floor in the corner and kicked it savagely.

"Chill," he warned himself. A solid workout would let him sort through his thoughts before the afternoon patient roster. He and Dr. Ma ran around Central Park this morning but he needed a greater level of exertion. She was always calm. He was always a bundle of nervous energy. So he trained. And trained. And trained.

Pulling on his usual snug workout briefs, an athletic cup, and nothing else, he padded out into the center of the main training room to stretch and meditate. It was nice to have the space to himself. It was usually crowded with students and sometimes onlookers in the gallery.

His body felt as it it was vibrating when he tried to become still in his meditation. Growling in frustration, he rose to his feet and began an ingrained moving meditation. He started with Qigong and segued into a very old Tai Chi form.

Leaping into the air and turning to land delicately on one foot, the other fully extended, he made his way through the series of gravity defying movements. They didn't teach this form in class. The athleticism and power required to accomplish it were almost beyond the average human being.

Crouching, kicking, punching and spinning his muscular frame rippled with the effort. Sweat rivulets traced their way around body landmarks as he moved, spilling in glistening droplets onto the floor. His golden tanned skin flushed darkly and his respirations increased.

Despite his best efforts, his thoughts kept creeping back to the events of the past forty eight hours. Realizing he was moving through the form in a blur of activity, he stopped, almost shaking with frustration.

He crossed quickly to the long wall of weapons. Carefully hung on ornate wooden hooks and arranged according to type and size, an incredible array of wooden practice implements were displayed.

He and Dr. Ma had their own private weapons in their office, but he didn't bother to retrieve his. Anything would do for the moment. Grabbing two Shinai, one short and one long, he returned to the center of the room to duplicate the same Tai Chi form.

The Shinai, mock swords made of four bamboo slats held together by leather fittings, made a slight whistling sound in the air as he added them to the form. He was not a weapons master, Dr. Ma was. David fought with his hands and body.

Holding and manipulating the Shinai helped him to focus. His movements were less instinctive. Still, he increased in speed and ferocity as he progressed. Out of the corner of his vision, he saw a movement. He could smell Jet Carlson, one of their student teachers, as she entered the dojo.

Their student teachers had access to the dojo at will. "She is probably surprised to see me in the middle of the day," he thought. Finishing the form again, he stopped, quietly replacing the two bamboo swords on the weapons wall.

Walking to where Jet sat in the gallery, patiently waiting for him to finish, he bowed to her. She returned his gesture, deeper and holding it longer. "We just returned from out of Town," he said in explanation. "I hope I wasn't interfering with a training you had planned."

Jet looked at him in surprise. "I would watch you practice that form all day Sifu," she said. I can't believe my good fortune."

David blushed slightly at her compliment. Her father, uncle and grandfather were famous martial arts practitioners. Jet had been studying with he and Dr. Ma for years at her male relative's insistence. One uncle was a very proficient Reiki Master as well.

David had always thought that her uncle knew what Dr. Ma and he really were, and that is why he encouraged Jet to train with them.

"You overstate my skill," he replied. It was the correct answer. The polite and self effacing answer of a great master.

Jet reached out a small towel to him. He wrapped it around his neck and face to dry off then realized he should probably just head to the shower. "Thank you," he said and turned to leave.

"David," she said hesitantly, calling him by name.

He turned back to her, surprised. He caught her gaze on the intricate tattoos wrapping his waist and abdomen before diving down into the snug workout shorts he wore. She felt him looking and raised her eyes quickly to his face.

"I'm sorry for staring," she apologized.

"No you are not," he said quietly. Jet was a very self confident young woman. Her martial arts skills were strong, thanks to her family lineage and her position as their student instructor.

"You are right," she agreed. I am not." They both laughed. "One day you will tell me the meaning?" she said pointing to his abdomen.

"Your grandfather knows," he replied.

"He told me what he thinks," she admitted. "I would like to hear the story from you." Before he could answer her, she continued. "Sosam is leaving the school."

David looked at her in surprise. "I wanted to catch you before class tonight," she said. "He is planning on telling you afterwards. His scholarship finally came in to attend USC."

"University of Southern California?" David said. "That's great. I will miss him of course. Wait, why is it so important for you to tell me before class?"

Jet looked at him. She seemed on the edge of telling him, but afraid to jump off. "He, well, he," she stumbled.

"Come on Jet," David said. "You are never at a loss for words. You and Sosam are thick as thieves. You came here to betray his confidence. It must be important."

"He knows he won't be coming back Sifu," she said, her voice full of hidden meaning. "Don't go out to the club for a good-bye drink with him. You are too nice to say no, most of the time."

David frowned, and then her meaning hit him. There was an iron clad rule of absolutely no intimacy with students, ever. Sosam had been open about his interest in him for years. "Why would he think his leaving would make a difference?" he said

Jet looked away. "I don't know," she said. "I just wanted to give you a heads up." She turned to walk back towards the locker rooms.

"Jet," David said, taking a step towards her. "I would rather you not tell anyone about watching me practice today. It wasn't the best example of Tai Chi form."

Jet considered for a moment and shook her head in agreement. "It was a perfect example of the form in use. I could have gotten a million hits on Youtube if I posted a video." She smiled at him as he paled a bit. "Kidding," she said. "That would be a disaster. Nobody human moves like that."

He watched her walk away, knowing she knew more than he ever wanted her to know. She was right. Nobody human. He headed to the dojo showers. He had a private bath in the Clinic, but he wanted to be dressed professionally before he went back and apologized to Winnie for his earlier behavior.

Winnie wasn't a fan of him coming to work all sweaty anyway.

After showering and dressing, he left Jet practicing quietly in the dojo. He would see her at class later. Opening the back door, his sharp tiger sense of smell picked up the Joy's takeout Winnie had ordered for lunch.

Walking up behind her as she was placing the takeout containers on the reception area table, he wrapped his arms around her ample waist in a tight hug.

"I'm sorry for this morning Winnie," he said. "I wasn't polite. Thank you for lunch, I don't know what I would do without you."

"Don't get all mushy on me boy," Winnie said with affection, patting his arms then pushing him away. "We all get an off day now and then," she said kindly. Turning to look at him more closely, she put her hands on his shoulders and said, "What is eating you? You are usually all smiles. Very annoying."

Tears formed in his eyes and splashed down onto his face as he turned away, embarrassed. Winnie looked surprised. She tugged him down to sit next to her on the couch. "Now, now," she said, patting his leg. "Nothing is forever."

David put his head in his hands, elbows propped on his knees. He looked absolutely miserable. "You are right," he answered her, his voice thick with emotion. "Nothing is that bad, but you are also wrong, many things are forever."

"Well you are going to just eat your lunch and get it together mister," she answered in her best task master voice. "We have patients and class tonight. Bud is working late, so I am coming to class and I expect your best!"

David smiled and shook his head. "I love you Winnie," he said softly. "You're right." He turned and wrapped his long arms around her for another brief hug. "Catch me up on everything I need to know. Dr. Ma is meeting with Detective Brenner about the recent murder victim. She may be delayed in getting here."

They both tucked into the fresh and fragrant meals from Joy's Happy Noodle Restaurant. The unique Thai fusion food was their favorite takeout. David always received a massive serving of mixed vegetables, lightly steamed with herbs. The restaurant owner, Joy herself, refused to send him raw fare.

"Easier to digest steamed," she always told him when he had the audacity to ask her *again* not to cook his meal. David would give up and accept the steamed food until he felt it was safe to ask again.

Winnie had just unlocked the front door after clearing away the remnants of their lunch when the first patient arrived. David was in his office going over charts when she popped her head around the door. "Room One is ready," she said. "I suggest you check that face in the mirror and reapply your usual smile before going in."

David knew she wouldn't let up until he snapped out of his self imposed funk. "Thank you Winnie, be right there," he replied.

Grabbing his lab coat, he slipped it on and stepped into the connecting hallway. He looked down, and briefly flashed back to kneeling on the floor struggling to hold Dr. Ma's Spirit Wind vision. "Was it just days ago? he thought. "Things are moving quickly with this case."

He took another step and faltered. A mark on the baseboard caught his eye. He knelt down and bent forward. There was a tiny symbol burned into the wood. Clearly visible against the cream colored paint, it appeared to be a infinity symbol.

David shook his head, puzzled. "How long has that been there and who left it?" he thought uneasily. He felt nothing malevolent about the mark, nor did he see, smell or hear any changes in the Clinic as a whole. He would show it to Dr. Ma when she arrived later.

In Room One, David greeted Terry, a retired world class Ironman competitor. The man, and his wife Marla, were good friends of Dr. Ma. "What's up bro?" Terry said as David entered the room.

David smiled. If anyone could put you in a good mood it was Terry. At sixty five years young, the man was a dynamo of activity. Training daily and still competing, Terry was in better shape than most people less than half his age.

"Hey Terry," David greeted him. "I'm sorry Dr. Ma isn't here, but tell me what is going on and I will take care of you the best I can."

"Just a quick checkup," Terry answered. "Nothing wrong, couldn't be better, but Dr. Ma won't keep giving me that voodoo juice she makes unless I come in."

David laughed. They had to see a patient every ninety days in person to keep them on any prescriptive herbal formula. Terry grumbled about coming in, but Dr. Ma had turned around a serious physical decline for him three years ago and he was enjoying his wins again.

"Okay Terry, I will keep you in her good graces," David said. "You look great. I understand you are on the podium in most races these days."

"Yep, yep," Terry said. "Except for the Mount Evans Hill Climb I just did. Got my ass handed to me. I was two hours behind what I expected to do it in, but I got it done. One more check off the bucket list."

David finished his tongue, pulse and range of motion exam of the fit, older man. "Long term, that's all that matters," he said.

"You could have gone with me," Terry teased. "You are thirty years younger than me. It would have been a piece of cake!"

"I don't know how to ride a bike," David said honestly.

"Don't know how to ride a bike?" Terry said. "That's crazy. I can get you up and going in no time. Didn't you have a bike as a kid?"

David flushed slightly, thinking of his less than normal childhood. Actually, a millennia of less than normal childhoods. "No," he said. "Dr. Ma wants me to ride the 'Loop Around The Lake' this year, but I just figure I will run it."

"In traffic?" Terry said, raising his eyebrows incredulously. "I will get you riding, I taught my kids, but we need a big enough bike. I can't lend you one of mine," he laughed. Terry was 5'6" to David's 6'5" frame.

"I will see what I can do," David said, walking him out to the front desk. "Hey Sam," he greeted the man sitting on the reception area couch.

Samuel Lightner smiled and stood to greet them. "Hey Doc! HeyTerry," Lightner said, "Terry, you aren't dead yet?"

"Nope," Terry answered. "Still hanging in there. When are you and David running Western States?"

He was referring to the one hundred mile endurance run from Squaw Valley to Auburn, California. Lightner had been trying to get David to go with him for several years.

"Two weeks," Sam answered. "We are supposed to leave a few days ahead, if David doesn't change his mind."

David cocked his head, smiling. He enjoyed the good natured teasing from the other two men. "I am ready," he said quietly. The race was not too much of a challenge for his abilities, despite the fact that he had refused Sam's offer to train together.

It was best sometimes to keep certain things under wraps. A few runs of that length and intensity that didn't debilitate him might raise unnecessary questions.

"You better be ready young man," Terry said to David. "Sam will leave you solo out there if you can't keep up."

"Yes," David nodded. "I understand, and rightly so."

Winnie cleared her throat. "Two more patients Dr. Anderson," she said to David, looking pointedly at the group. "Not counting Mr. Lightner here."

"I'm just here to get my herbal prescription Winnie," Sam said guiltily. "I was waiting to speak to Dr. David for a moment."

"You will have one hundred miles to talk in a couple weeks," Winnie said shortly. "If the doctor will sign your chart, I will get you checked out. You too Mr. Cappello," she said to Terry.

Chapter Ten - Winnie Quits Her Job

While David handled matters at the Clinic, Dr. Ma and Allistair arrived at her residence off Flagler Drive.

Mort had arrived home before they did. A light lunch was already spread out on the kitchen island. Pasta salad, fruit and fresh bread accompanied a glass of Chardonnay for Allistair and sparkling water for Dr. Ma.

They both greeted Detective Brenner as he arrived. Mort rolled his eyes as the detective sat down and quickly filled a plate to overflowing. He began to eat with the two Elementals.

"Thanks for the lunch invite Dr. Ma," Jeremy said around his first mouthful. "This is delicious, I have been living on takeout and snacks."

"I thought you were getting thin," she responded. "David thought it was because of some other distraction."

Jeremy Brenner's Irish heritage gave him the ability to turn bright red for a moment when embarrassed. He did so now as he looked away, trying to hide his response. "Oh, no, I am working out a bit more is all."

"Gracie is a nice young lady," Ma teased. Brenner turned scarlet again for a moment. "You seem to really like her."

"Let's talk about the case," the detective said, changing the subject. He reached for another helping of pasta salad. "The husband is our killer?" he asked.

"Looks like it," Allistair commented.

"What have we got in the way of evidence?" Brenner inquired. He had stopped eating and was scribbling away furiously on his pocket notepad.

"*Who* we have in the way of evidence is better that *what* we have," Dr. Ma answered him. "Are you actually using a paper notepad?" Allistair asked incredulously. Brenner just looked at him and shook his head.

"Yes," Ma said, "Jeremy is resistant to current electronic devices."

"Evidence," Jeremy reminded her without looking up from his writing.

"A friend in New York had a party that was attended by the victim the night she died," Dr. Ma explained. "There is surveillance video of someone poisoning her drink."

Brenner looked up surprised. "How do you know it was poison?"

"The killer wore gloves to break off a piece of art that becomes toxic when dissolved in liquids," she said. "He was seen later, handing the drink to the victim. Now that we know what the substance was, you will be able to run a toxicology screen for it."

"Too obscure for a routine test I assume," Brenner said.

"Very obscure," Allistair said, pouring himself a second glass of Chardonnay.

"How did she get to the party?" the detective asked.

"She approached our friend's social secretary," Dr. Ma replied. "Evidently the victim and her husband wanted to give a similar party and she was doing research. The secretary will give a full statement."

"I'm afraid the identity of the man giving the party will not be revealed," Allistair added. "Everything he has to share with law enforcement will be given freely of course, but not his name."

Brenner frowned. "How did she get left here in Palm Beach, frozen?"

Dr. Ma looked at Allistair before answering. "We haven't figured that part out yet and may never. We do have the killer dragging her on surveillance from the party area on the roof to the other side where the maintenance sheds are."

"So, Jeremy said, "We need to get a confession from the hired killer?"

"Well, Dr. Ma said. "The killer may have gotten away. How about trying a setup on the husband? If he doesn't know the killer is in the wind, maybe a little blackmail will get him to implicate himself."

"Interesting," Brenner said. "He is here in Palm Beach, arranging for a service for Bridgette on their yacht in a few days. What do you have in mind?"

Dr. Ma and Allistair outlined the plan they had developed on the trip home to Detective Brenner.

"I will wait to see what I get from this little Op before I share with NYPD. I have been officially loaned to them anyway. The medical examiner's time of death seems closer to the victim's probable arrival here than your rooftop party's time line. Maybe the poison took awhile to work," Brenner said.

"Maybe so," Ma agreed. "Allistair is my friend's solicitor. Go with him to his office and he will get you everything you need, that we can offer."

"Thanks," Jeremy said, standing abruptly. "Ready?" the said to the stocky attorney.

"Yes," Allistair grumbled, downing the last of his wine and standing up. "Everybody is in a rush these days."

Dr. Ma smiled and walked them to the door. "I am going to the Clinic now, let me know if you need anything else from me Jeremy."

"Will do," Brenner shot over his shoulder as he half jogged out to his car.

The meticulous attorney followed behind him, grumbling to himself.

Allistair's driver held open his door and the fussy man got in, shooting Dr. Ma one last look of frustration at having to rush.

Mort appeared at her shoulder as she closed the door. "Will you and David be needing anything tonight?" he asked. "I am thinking of taking a few hours off."

Dr. Ma looked surprised. "Really? How unusual," she said. "Are you going to visit Nidi?" She knew Mort had been visiting David's ancient Djinn now and then since she had stayed in the Library during their last case.

She wasn't sure if he was helping her care for David or just interested in getting to know the ancient creature. Nidi knew everything about everything Djinn. She had belonged to Kaia, David's Elemental mother, a powerful and even more ancient being with obscure origins.

"Perhaps," Mort said cagily.

"Say hello," Ma said as she grabbed her briefcase and headed out the door. She needed to get some actual work done. Winnie would be getting frustrated over the backlog at the Clinic. Besides, she would co-teach with David tonight, for both their sakes.

The Tiger was not having a good week. Too much coming at him from different angles. He wasn't at his best, and she wasn't helping matters much. She thought he would jump at the chance to interact with her on the beach. She forgot that his love for her may prevent him from thinking her offer of a casual sexual encounter was all that interesting.

Ma sighed as she got in her Mars red, Mercedes C63 AMG Coupe and headed towards the Clinic. She really liked this car. So did David, but he didn't drive. His natural color blindness and limitation in daytime vision accuracy from his tiger genes, precluded her feeling safe if he did.

Samuel Lightner and Terry Capello were standing the parking lot, talking animatedly, when Dr. Ma pulled in. She parked the car and walked up to them. "How are my two favorite athletes?"

All three of them laughed. Everyone was Dr. Ma's favorite athlete. Her patients were like an extended family.

"Great!" Terry said, holding out his paper bag filled with supplements and an herbal formula. "Just stocking up on my voodoo stuff so I can keep up with these young men," he said, indicating Sam.

"David cleared you?" Dr. Ma asked. "Your appointment was at 3:00 PM. It is barely 3:30, no *electrocution*?"

Terry called Dr. Ma's routine acupuncture, plus electrical stimulation treatment, his 'electrocution session.' The older man shook his head in the negative. "Nope, must have thought I didn't need it."

Ma rolled her eyes. "He's fired," she said smiling. "What about you Sam?"

The tall, lean, endurance runner held up a similar bag. "Thank you for getting this ready for me. Speaking of ready, has David been training for Western States?"

Dr. Ma noted that both men were looking at her skeptically. They wanted reassurance that

David would be ready to compete when he flew out to California with Sam.

"Does he look like he isn't training?" Dr. Ma asked.

"That doesn't answer my question," Samuel Lightner said seriously. "He always looks like some sort freak of nature from a fitness perspective. It's his first hundred mile race, and the course is really grueling."

"You are still packing his gear, providing a ground crew and dressing him, right?" Dr. Ma asked him.

"Yes," he answered, surprised. "Of course. He has no idea what to bring. I even bought him trail shoes, but I don't think he has even worn them. They looked new when I picked them up to pack."

"As long as you are with him Sam," she said, "he will be fine. You don't know how tough he is. I wouldn't worry about it."

"In that case," Terry said, looking at Sam, "a little wager should be in order. I bet dinner with the wives he will beat you to the finish."

Lighter's face clouded over. "You're on bud," he said. "He will be lucky if he finishes, but there is no way in hell he will beat me."

Dr. Ma laughed and shook her head as she walked in the Clinic's back door. They were still arguing happily about possibilities as the door shut, closing out the sound of their voices.

David met her in the hallway. "Is that Sam and Terry still out there in the parking lot?" he asked her.

"Yes," she said. "They are arguing about whether you will even make it to the finish at Western States and betting dinner on the outcome."

David grinned. "I will have to make it look like I am suffering a bit for realism. I am not however, letting Sam win. I will leave him behind at the finish line just to shut him up."

Dr. Ma smiled. "I am sure you will, Tiger."

David flushed. He didn't want her to think he was being overly competitive with humans who couldn't match him in strength and ability. "I'm just going to get him to stop bugging me about running these races with him."

"Why?" she said. "I think you may enjoy it. Wait until you see how it goes before you decide not to go again. Definitely beat Sam, but don't prejudge another race."

David looked at her for a moment. He felt uneasy about her change in attitude towards him lately. Something like the race could open an opportunity for unwelcome discovery as an Elemental. She usually discouraged that kind of activity. Activity that brought danger.

Danger for him. Something else she was usually against. She hadn't even insisted on coming with him, or sending Allistair.

"Okay," he said. "I guess I should run the distance at least once in a public way to give Sam some peace of mind. There is nothing organized, but that patient of your who does ultras, said he runs 70-80 miles on Saturdays along the coast. I'll call him about it this weekend."

"I will make sure Jeremy doesn't need us for anything and bike along with you," she said.

He gave her another long look before asking about the mark on the baseboard. "Have you seen this?" he said pointing it out.

He watched her bend down to look. Her face paled slightly. "No, I haven't seen it," she said. He could tell she was avoiding telling him something.

"What is it?" he asked her directly. She looked at him. Knowing she couldn't easily lie, she said, "It is a Spirit mark."

"Yes?" he prompted. He saw her shifting uncomfortably, not wanting to tell him but unable to find a plausible fabrication.

It probably came the night you struggled to hold that Spirit Wind for me, she admitted finally. "Between Pazuzu, the Lamassu and the magician, Bridgette's death was highly charged, so to say."

"That is the overwhelming zap I got trying to help you?" he asked.

"Exactly," she said. "That you got, not me. You aren't as strong as you could be David." He started to say something but she just pulled him into her office and closed the door. Her hand was placed lightly over his mouth.

"Not so loud," she said. "Let's not add carelessness to the rest of the things that went wrong this week. I know you didn't like my solution on the beach to make you stronger. You don't really have a choice. Your weakness is becoming a liability."

David stiffened. "I'm not weak, even if I am not as strong as Avo was," he said slowly, frowning. "But I don't have to accept your offer of recreational sex either. You don't want to have the relationship with me that you had with Avo. I get it."

"No, I don't want the same type of relationship," she agreed. "But, I am willing to help you get stronger," she started to say.

"Don't," he said, cutting her off. "I feel about as bad as I am going to without you reinforcing that I am one of your charities. Accept me as I am. If I die, I'll be back. You have others to help you in the interim. Maybe with a little luck, a newer version of me is coming and you can relax a bit. I have noticed you are less protective lately. Good for both of us."

She just stared at him, unsure of how to respond. This conversation was going downhill, no stopping it. "David," she began.

He held up a hand, "Stop," he said. "Stop talking about it. I will meet you in the dojo for class." He turned and walked out the back door.

Winnie was sitting at her desk, humming softly. Dr. Ma knew it was her nervous habit when the two of them were having a serious discussion. Somehow the humming would drown out any possibility of overhearing them.

"No more patients?" Ma asked her. She noticed Winnie had locked the front door and turned the sign to closed.

"The last two cancelled Dr. Ma," her assistant said without looking up. "Did David take some snacks with him? I didn't receive a request to order dinner for after the class."

"I'm not sure if he did," Dr. Ma answered her. "I'm sure he will grab some from the mini fridge in the office there. Are you coming to class?"

"I was," Winnie said, "but Bud isn't feeling well and I am going to go home to check on him."

"Let me know if there is something I can do," Ma said to her. Winnie's husband Bud was a cancer survivor. Changes to his health were always watched carefully. Working for Dr. Ma had its benefits for Winnie in healthy eating and easy access to alternative medical care.

Winnie looked up briefly. "Dr. Ma," she said. "I wanted to speak with you about my position here."

Ma noticed the odd tone in her assistants voice. "Yes?" she said, sitting on one of the pharmacy stools behind Winnie's desk.

"Bud and I are getting older and we would like to live closer to our grandchildren," Winnie said. "My daughter's husband just got a promotion and they are moving to a bigger house in the suburbs with a guest cottage. It may be perfect for Bud and I."

"So you are going to move then," Dr. Ma said.

"Yes," Winnie replied in her clipped and efficient tone. "I would like to stay until we get a suitable replacement for me, but a month would be the longest I can wait."

Dr. Ma nodded, careful not to express any surprise or emotion. Winnie had been a stellar employee. She didn't want the woman to be concerned about leaving; they would manage. Or she would. She wasn't sure about David at the moment.

"Place ads please," she told Winnie. "We can begin interviews right away. Don't be concerned about whether we find the right replacement. Make plans to go and I will manage regardless."

Winnie gave her a relieved look and smiled. Quitting had weighted heavily on her mind. She knew that Dr. Ma and David depended on her. "I'll talk to Bud tonight," she said. "We will set the move for four weeks, but be ready to go sooner. Thank you."

"Let me know if I can do anything to make the transition easier Winnie," Ma said. "I have to get to class." The elegant woman stood up and headed across the clinic towards the back door exit. "Give my best to Bud."

"Will do," came the reply behind her.

Dr. Ma exited the back door and into the Zen garden that surrounded the space between the clinic rear entrance and the martial arts school rear entrance. A full moon shone brightly through the gazebo lattice, despite the fact that it was just dusk.

The light from the moon would be incredible tonight in full darkness. She knew suddenly that she needed to fly. There was someone who had the answer to several burning questions and they were very far away. "David can handle class by himself," she thought.

Jet Carlson had just parked her car, arriving for class early as usual. When she walked up to Dr. Ma, the older woman said, "Jet, can you tell David I won't be in class tonight? Neither will Winnie I'm afraid."

Jet really like the Clinic's manager. She always spent extra time when Winnie attended class.

"Of course Sensei," Jet replied, with a slight bow of her head. "I can assist Sifu David," she caught herself for a moment, realizing she was being a bit presumptuous to replace Dr. Ma with her limited skills. "If he needs anything of course," she finished, stumbling a bit.

"You are very capable of assisting David, Jet," her teacher answered. "Would you give him a ride home for me?"

Jet paused, her cheeks coloring. "I will Sensei, of course, but I think Sosam wants to give him a ride, home that is, tonight." The younger woman broke off, unsure how much to reveal to Dr. Ma.

"What is going on Jet? Spill," Dr. Ma said frowning slightly.

"Sosam is leaving the dojo, Sensei," Jet explained nervously. "I told Sifu David earlier that he might be asking him to go out for a, uh, drink tonight to say goodbye."

"You mean you warned David that Sosam might pressure him to have sex based on the affection Sosam has had for David? That seems short sighted. Sosam is just going to college. Does he mean to never come back to the Mugen Dojo?"

"I think his judgement is a bit cloudy right now," Jet answered truthfully.

"Watch out for Sifu David tonight, if you would," Ma told her. "He will choose to give Sosam what he wants. He is a gentle soul your teacher. It bothers him to see anyone distraught."

"But then Sosam is banned from returning to the school," Jet burst out. She stopped herself, remembering who she was speaking to. "I'm sorry Sensei," she said, lowering her head. "That is his choice."

"Yes Jet," Dr. Ma said softly. Sadness washed over her. "So many changes," she thought. Something big on the horizon. Time to fly.

"Well, thank you Jet for keeping an eye on your teacher tonight. You and your wife deserve a night out anyway, right? Is Sosam planning on the Colony Hotel?"

"Probably," Jet said, her cheeks coloring again. Dr. Ma and David were so accepting of everyone around them. When she married her longtime partner last year, they both came to the wedding and gave them a very generous gift.

Jet always figured it was some Universal design that managed to give Sifu David and Sensei Ma two gay teaching assistants. None of the students seemed to mind, if they even knew. The no fraternization with teaching staff thing was iron clad in the Mugen Dojo. That was why Sosam would have to leave if he and David were intimate tonight.

"Enjoy then," Ma said, turning towards her car. "I will see you at class later this week."

Jet watched Dr. Ma walk away. "That was an interesting conversation," she thought as she hurried in the dojo's back door. The older woman always seemed to know everything. Sometimes it was unnerving.

Chapter Eleven - Different Directions

Jet delivered Dr. Ma's message to David, then hurried to the unisex changing area. Even the showers were gender inclusive. Privacy panels and individual shower stalls with thick curtains gave everyone the anonymity they needed. The strong vein of respect among the students gave another layer.

David was still flustered by Sosam Li's quiet announcement to him before class, that this would be his last time at the school. He was glad Jet had given him a heads up this afternoon. Sosam had left a message yesterday asking David if they could go the the Colony Hotel tonight after class for his birthday. David had taken him there before for dinner and drinks.

"Exactly as Jet said," David said to himself softly when the younger man walked away to prepare for class. Tonight was an advanced class. Multiple forms were used in mock, but realistic fight sequences. Dr. Ma was usually here to provide a second pair of eyes. Not tonight.

David would use Jet and Sosam as his demonstration pair and move among the students solo as they practiced the complex sequences. The intense level of concentration that would require, would allow him a brief respite from everything that was working itself out in his head.

He was glad Winnie wasn't coming, even though he wondered why. They never kept her from attending any classes she could manage the time for. Tonight would be much simpler with all advanced students and him teaching solo.

The front door opened to admit Gracie and Jeremy Brenner. Gracie headed towards the changing area while Jeremy hurried over to David. "Evening." he said with an easy smile. "Okay if I take this class tonight? Gracie asked me to come. She said I was too involved in work lately."

David paused for a moment, then said, "Yes, of course Jeremy. I am surprised to see you. This will be Gracie's first time here as well, despite the fact I have encouraged her to come." "Thanks!" Brenner said cheerfully. "Where is Dr. Ma?" he said, looking around.

"She is taking care of another business matter," David said carefully. "I will be solo tonight."

"Oh," Brenner said, surprised. "I wanted to tell her that the Op we discussed today is set for tomorrow night, if you two are available."

David paused, not wanting to reveal too much to the eager cop. "She and I were too busy to discuss your lunch meeting, and then she had to leave ah, rather suddenly. I'm sorry I am not up to date. I will be there of course."

Brenner looked at David shrewdly. "And Dr. Ma?"

David flushed slightly, caught by the quick detective being too vague in his answers. "She will have to let you know. I don't have any idea how complicated the issue she is dealing with will become." He turned away before Brenner could come up with any more questions.

Pulling a black wicking t-shirt over his head with the school logo, David went to stand at the front of the room. He had pulled on a pair of full length training tights as soon as the teaching assistants Sosam and Jet arrived.

David trained solo at the school in a snug pair of running briefs and a supportive cup. For class he dressed professionally. His array of unusual tattoos, scars, and his muscular physique was more of a distraction to students than anything else. Or so Dr. Ma had told him. He had a bad habit of being oblivious to certain things until they hit him in the face.

This was part of the weakness the dragon had been on him about lately. He wasn't always aware enough to avoid near mortal danger. He also missed quite a few social interaction clues until it was too late. Hence his nearly non existent dating life.

The students paired off eagerly. This was a monthly class. Nothing like it was held at any other local school. Using Jet and Sosam as his demonstration models, David worked his way through a complex series of fight sequences.

A few times he thought he caught an odd expression on his male teaching assistant's face. "He is sad," David thought. "Well, life is full of choices. Our decisions define us."

The last sequence began with Karate. In the advanced class, multiple styles flowed in and out of the sequences. The students let loose with a flurry of punches and blocks.

Shifting to Tai Chi, each pair became fluid and graceful after their concrete statue-like beginning. Feet struck and circled, bodies slid and leaned while graceful hand and arm movements collided with sudden sharp cracks.

Finally, the teaching pair, dove for strategically placed Shinai and moved backward and forward in a linear format. The bamboo practice swords were snapping and cracking with each blow. The student pairs followed in suit.

"Stop," David said clearly in English. It was Gracie and Jeremy's first time and he didn't want to confuse them. Usually and Dr. Ma spoke Japanese or Mandarin to the students to give them a sense of traditional training.

The pairs broke apart and all the students turned inward to face him. He was at the center of a large circle of armed opponents. David grinned. The advanced students grinned back. Jet looked at Gracie and Jeremy and quietly mouthed, "Follow our lead," indicating she and Sosam Li.

"Hajime!" David shouted suddenly. There was a flurry of activity as each pair of students attempted to engage the tall man at their center. Holding no weapon, David seemed to be elated by their sudden attacks.

Dodging, turning, parrying with his hands and feet, he avoided every blow directed at him. Within minutes, most of the students were breathing too hard to continue at the original pace and stepped back.

Jet and Sosam faced him alone. A loud yell from Sosam began their onslaught. Jet rolled forward and to the side, slicing her Shinai towards David's feet from a kneeling position as Sosam charged him head on.

David calmly slipped his shirt over his head and wrapped the fabric around Sosam's hands on the weapon's hilt. Launching himself up and over his male attacker he used Li's forward momentum to propel him. Almost lifting Li from the ground, David slammed him down on his back on the padded practice surface.

Jet's blade met empty space where David's feet had been. As she rolled to the side to avoid David landing on her, he came to rest in the same location he started, bending over her, his hand bladed at her throat. Sosam was weaponless, still struggling to catch his breath after the impact of his fall.

David helped both assistants to their feet. Stepping back and bowing, the final three ended the mock conflict. Clapping erupted from the assembly of students. David smiled and bowed giving them the same respect for their efforts.

The students drifted off the floor to put their weapons away and clean the school before leaving. David walked back to the private office he shared with Dr. Ma to shower and change. His laser focus for class was quickly replaced with his concern over Sosam Li and tonight's invitation.

Walking back to the dojo floor, he saw Li waiting for him. Everyone else was gone. Sosam walked up to him and smiled. "Ready?" he asked shyly putting his hand on David's shoulder.

"As I ever will be," David thought. Aloud he said, "Sure, let's go."

Dr. Ma reached her home off Flagler Drive in record time. "I am lucky I didn't get a ticket for driving that fast," she thought. She hurriedly parked. Touching the security rune on the front door, she rushed through the house to her bedroom. She quickly changed to black training gear. Then she went out the patio doors into the darkening evening.

As expected, the moon was growing brighter with each passing hour. The hot and humid South Florida night sky was devoid of any clouds. Berenice greeted her as she rushed past. "Good evening!" the statue called after her.

"Evening!" Ma replied distractedly. Reaching the concrete barrier wall at the end end of her property where it held back the Intracoastal Waterway, she leapt up and out. Transforming as she reached her arms wide, she gave several powerful thrusts of her massive wing span and rose upward.

Directly towards the brightening moon she flew. "Allistair!" she called silently as she rose. "Are you tracking me?"

"Of course," came his disgruntled reply. "Are you sure this is the best course of action right now?" he asked.

"Trust me," she said, rising higher and higher.

Dr. Ma had called her old friend en-route home. "Please go to the Library tonight and tell Maia to expect my body to appear for a bit of time." Maia would know how to maintain her human body while she was gone.

Maia had maintained the contents and Berenice the security of the library for millennia. Bernice, or Queen Berenice II of Egypt, wife of Ptolemy III Euergetes had a vested interest. She and her long dead King reigned when Alexandria had become an important cultural center.

Maia on the other hand was bored with immortality and truly loved the contents of the Library. She had recently started a shelf of *People Magazines*. Dr. Ma wasn't thrilled with that decision

Only Allistair, David, Maia and Mort knew that Ma could travel through different planes of existence, but had to leave her human body behind. Her human form would show up in the Library when she broke through the dimensional barrier. Maia would wrap her in some of Allistair's shed skin in a sort of stasis until she got back, if needed.

It was a bit touchy as to how long she would be gone. She had gotten better at estimating time between dimensions through the last two millennia, but it wasn't a perfect science.

Especially where she intended to go this time. She was going home. She needed to speak with the creator about David. She wasn't sure she could actually get there, but she would ask David's mother Kaia for help. She needed answers.

She had a slight regret about leaving Jeremy in the middle of a murder case without her help, but David and Allistair were there. Besides, if all went well, she would be back in no time.

Higher and higher she flew towards the moon's glowing countenance. Ice crystals formed on her wings, she let go a massive fireball of breath ahead of her and flew through it, effectively de-icing herself.

"Kaia!" she intoned to the Universe at large. "I call you. Bring me to the creator." Nothing happened as she flew upward. Another de-icing came and went. She was feeling weary. Usually she crossed over by now. It was just a matter of focusing on her destination.

Except she didn't know her actual destination this time. She had only her vague memories of home to focus on. "Kaia!" she called again, a little more weakly. She did not want to give up. She needed to know the plan for David. Too much information was missing in the big picture.

Suddenly, pressure like a monstrous hand gripped her body, stopping her in mid flight. She didn't struggle. "No fear," she told herself. "Whatever happens is part of the master plan."

The pressure increased until she thought she would be crushed out of existence. Still she didn't struggle. She pushed any fear of pain or death from her thoughts. Following her instincts for over two millennia on Earth had brought her to this point.

Everything was the Universal plan. She cried out once as the pressure seemed to implode her Dragon's form and then nothingness took over her mind.

In the Library, Ma's human form slowly manifested on the floor of the room where Allistair and Maia were standing. They waited for her to become solid in every aspect. When her chest slowly rose and fell with steady breaths, they lifted her onto the chaise that had appeared for that very purpose.

"Well," Allistair observed. "She made it. I had my doubts."

"Now you tell me," Maia snapped at him. She placed a soft, wool blanket over Ma's unconscious figure and propped her head on a small down-filled pillow.

"No use in worrying everyone ahead of time," Allistair replied, draining the last of his glass of sherry.

"What will you tell David until she returns?" Maia said, looking at Dr. Ma with a worried expression.

"I'll cross that tooth and claw filled bridge if and when I come to it," he answered her. "Wrap her in the skin you have if she is not back in a few days. Use the IV and the oxygen mask if it gets prolonged."

"I know what I am doing," Maia said sighing. "I don't like this trip, but she has come through unscathed before. Just not from *that* location."

"I'm going home now," he announced. "It's my feeding time of the month and I am very hungry."

Maia made a shooing motion at him. "Off you go then. I will have Mort call you if anything changes."

Allistair walked over to Berenice's statue in the library and touched her shoulder. "Ready," he said. In moments he was standing in Dr. Ma's darkened garden. The brilliant glow of the full moon covered everything with a silvery blanket, darkening the undersides of plantings and structures deeper than they were without light.

A soft rumbling from Jamil came to the Snake's Elemental ears. "She made it safely I assume?"

Allistair grinned. The ancient Sentinel didn't miss a trick. "Yes Guardian," he said respectfully.

"I will watch for her return passage, in the event she has any difficulties," Jamil rumbled.

Shaking his head, Allistair wondered just how much power the ancient being possessed. More than any of them realized he would bet.

He looked up into the night sky before entering the back patio doors.

"Hurry back my dear," he said to himself as he walked through her house and out to his car in the driveway. "I am going to have a stressed out Tiger on my hands if you don't."

Allistair drove home while David and Sosam Li were arriving at the Colony Hotel in Palm Beach. Certain nights were known for a gathering of gay patrons and that is where Li had suggested they start the night.

"If this night with David was going to be the last time, he was going to enjoy it." Li thought. He had struggled with his decision since he made it, and confided his plan to Jet Carlson.

"You are a lunatic," she promptly told him. "Who gives up years of training and a friendship with one of the greatest martial arts teachers for a roll in the hay?"

"You don't understand," he had replied defensively. "I have been in love with him for years."

"Oh please!" she had laughed. "You and everyone else. Except me of course." Jet was only interested in women. "You are giving up years at the dojo and this will be a one time thing. He is not going to fall for you and follow you to school in California."

"You never know," he had replied hotly. He remembered her shaking her head at him incredulously and walking away.

David was dressed for a high end night out. Sosam couldn't breathe for a minute when he first saw him at the dojo. They had gone to dinner before. David was always dressed casual in jeans and a polo or button down and sport jacket.

Tonight he wore what appeared to be custom Armani. Li's mother was a buyer in men's fashion. Lightweight tropical wool pants and matching jacket, with the now popular again Neru collar. An off white silk crew neck shirt underneath set the look up for elegance with a modern touch. The Moreschi Metz Blue leather slip-ons made Li smile.

His mother would love this. David's friend, Barry, dressed him of course. The stunning man wore what Barry styled him in. His lean, muscled physique could make any fashion work well, but Barry always did chic and classic.

Sosam's self doubt evaporated as he took in his incredibly handsome date. David was flushing slightly at the inspection. He looked a bit unnerved, very unlike him. The younger man knew why. Another wave of doubt washed over him.

"Is this okay with you?" he asked David openly. "I don't want to be forcing anything on you."

"I know what you want out of tonight So," David used his nickname for his soon to be former student. "Let's just see how things go. I don't want to disappoint you. I'm definitely a little uncomfortable. When are you leaving?"

"I fly out tomorrow," Sosam answered quickly.

"Well that takes the pressure off," David laughed. He let Li lead the way out of the dojo's back door after arming the alarm.
Getting in Li's car, they drove towards Palm Beach.

Detective Brenner left class that night in a euphoric mood. The class was way more than he expected and Gracie shared his excitement. They were still talking and laughing animatedly by their cars after the other students had left.

"Would you like to get some coffee?" he asked her rather suddenly. It was now or never. He needed to ask her before he lost his nerve. She was younger than him, very driven towards her goal to compete in the Olympics in the martial arts and he seemed to get tongue tied when he saw her.

She hesitated, looking at him. "I have work in the morning and I have class," she began.

"No problem, of course," he said cutting her off before she could say she wasn't interested in him. Best to just get a polite refusal for reasons that were personal to her and not about rejecting him.

"Wait, no, I wasn't turning you down," she said. "I am pretty hungry and caffeine keeps me awake if I drink it this late. How about a quick bite down the street at the Thai place?"

Brenner was surprised. He answered quickly before she could change her mind. "I love Joy's. I am starved too. My treat?"

"Is this a date or just charity to a poor Olympic hopeful?" she laughed.

"A date," he said before he could talk himself out of it. "If that is okay with you? I am older than you and probably not as interesting as most," was all he got out before she kissed him lightly.

Taken completely off guard, he hesitated before kissing her back.

"I really like you Jeremy. You're not that old and boring, really," she said. "Actually, you are very sexy." She leaned into him, kissing him and running her hand over his hard muscled chest.

"We had better get going," he said a bit thickly. "Or you are not going to get any food tonight."

"Oh really Detective Brenner?" she said archly. He looked at her again, amazed that young women were so forward. He came from a solid Irish Catholic upbringing. Not that he wasn't thrilled. He was. Too thrilled. Definitely time for food.

"Follow me, or do you want me to drive you?" he said. He had his POV (personally owned vehicle) versus his agency issued unmarked car. He couldn't have offered her a ride in his police car for a date.

She looked at him a moment longer and said, "Let's drive together. We have class in the morning. If we happen to stay out all night. I can leave my car here and you can drive me back."

Jeremy opened the passenger door for her without saying a word. He probably couldn't have spoken if he tried. Her last comments had effectively frozen his tongue to the roof of his mouth in surprise.

Chapter Twelve - Dr. Ma And The Creator

The nothingness dissipated slowly. Fragments of thoughts wandered through her mind. Sensation was oddly muted. She tried to open her eyes and focus on an image, but things were very blurry. She waited patiently.

Where she was wasn't as important as the fact that she was somewhere other that where she had started. She had been successful in going either were she had intended, or where she was able to go. To speak with her Creator. David's Creator.

As the blurry edges solidified, she saw herself standing on the high mountain ledge she remembered from the very last time she saw home. The winding path up the mountain grew clearer. The rock of the mountain took on depth and color. Overhead a blazing sun lit the landscape from a bright blue sky.

Her Dragon form looked different here. Crisper, clearer. The form that was created here and belonged here. She always felt that her manifestation in the Earthly realm left something to be desired. For all Otherworldly beings. She felt more powerful here.

Her raptor vision picked out a small figure walking up the path towards her. "Was it him?" she thought. "After so long, it had to be him. She came all this way, risked so much to speak to him."

Another figure stepped out from behind a rock cleft nearby. She recognized her immediately. Kaia, David's mother. The womanly figure, sweet smile and an aura of kindness surrounded her. Deceiving at best.

Mother of the Earth, she was one of the most ancient and powerful beings in the Universe. "She just looks like someone's mom," Ma thought.

"Welcome Ama," she said in her gentle voice.

The Dragon knelt in front of her. "Thank you Great Mother for helping me get here."
Kaia frowned slightly. Ma shivered at the possibility that the powerful being was less than pleased with her actions. "What choice did I have?" Kaia said. "You were bound to be helped or let you destroy yourself. And, you have much more to do."

The small figure had drawn closer as they spoke. Kaia turned towards him, watching as he made his way to them. "My love," she greeted him as he approached them. Ma felt a sudden shock run through her.

"My love?" she thought. "Yes, I remember now. This is what it what was all about, saving Kaia's Earthly inhabitants." She noticed the vibrant energy around both Kaia and her creator merging and twisting between them. The closer he came to the smiling Earth mother, the faster the energy swirled, thickening and glittering in the light.

"Beautiful one," the seemingly ancient male being said to Ma. Smiling at her, he looked for all the world like any old man she had met on Earth. He held his hand out to stroke her shiny, black scaled shoulder. Something seemed off to her. She couldn't feel his touch.

"Am I home?" she said, "or is this just an illusion?"

"An illusion of course," he replied. "You cannot come home. At least not yet. I am only here in spirit."

"Will you answer my questions about David?" she said. She didn't mean to sound brusque, but there was no need to delay. She didn't even know if and when she would make it back to the Earthly realm.

"You want to know who he is, why he seems weak and if he will die soon," her creator said, ticking off each point on his ancient and gnarled fingers.

"Yes, Great Master," she replied respectfully.

The old man sat on a small boulder at the edge of the cliff. He looked at her for a long moment and then at Kaia. She nodded an answer to some silent communication between the two of them.

"David is the last Tiger, not one of many," he said. "Kaia's Earth priestesses spent the thousand years you were with Avo breeding the perfect human being to die and be reborn as your opposite." He took a breath and looked out on the glittering day around them. He smiled grimly.

Turning back to her, he said, "David was born to suffer at the hands of humans each time he comes back to the world. He will always be born into abuse and anger, and after you find him, spend another lifetime struggling with his sensitivity and compassion."

Kaia looked at her. "The weakness you see in him is his great strength. He is your complete opposite. No matter what you think, he is the perfect mate for your energies."

"That is why he gets stronger when you interact with him intimately," her creator said. "And why you get weaker. You felt it after that first time, lethargy while you flew."

"It is the ultimate balance," Kaia added. "You represent Otherworldly beings, he represents the human race."

Ma said nothing while they spoke with her. There was nothing to say. She came to ask, and to listen. They had stopped talking. She felt this was all she was going to get from them.

"Thank you," she said bowing to them. "I will think about what you have said and try to better accomplish the purpose I was created for."

She looked up, but they were gone. So fast! Around her the crisp and clear images began to fade. Before long, nothingness reasserted its hold. She relaxed into its embrace.

When sensation returned, she was lying on a chaise in the Library. Not moving, she allowed the full recovery of all her senses. Opening her eyes, she saw Maia sitting next to her in a Louis XIV chair, reading a *People Magazine*.

"Hello Maia," she said. The beautiful Spirit woman, very substantial in the Library dimension, almost fell out of the chair in shock. Her magazine went flying and she grasped at her chest. One that hadn't moved in millennia for any purpose that a human being needed it to. Not to breathe, nor speak.

"Ma-sama!" she cried happily. Bending over the Elemental on the chaise, the tiny Spirit hugged her fiercely. "Welcome back!"

"Thank you Maia," Ma said. "It's good to see you, but more importantly, how long have I been gone?"

Maia looked disconcerted for a moment, then she understood the question. "Less than twelve hours. It is about 10: 00 AM the morning after you left."

Thank goodness for days off," Ma thought. Winnie had been against them from the day Dr. Ma had instituted them.

"Bad for business," she had expressed to Dr. Ma.

Lately Ma was thrilled with the policy that gave her and David one day off from the Clinic and Dojo each week together and one day off a week separately. Living for eternity, you would think, gave them plenty of time to do what they wanted or needed.

That was not the case. The days off were lifesavers. They were both off today. She wondered how David was spending his day and if he knew she had been gone. Tonight they were supposed to help Jeremy with his sting to catch Bridgette Cohen's husband. She didn't want to miss that.

She rose slowly from the chaise and let Maia help her to Berenice's stone statue. "Hello Ma-sama!" the immortal woman said from her statue's stone mouth Her lapis blue eyes opened. All Otherworldly beings had the same color eyes. It was a tell, if you knew what to look for. "Ready to go?"

Ma nodded, placing one hand on the statue's shoulder. In a moment, she was standing in the garden behind her residence. The statue and it's fountain were merrily gurgling away, spraying water in every direction to attract birds to the yard.

She looked around, again wanting to connect with David, but not wanting to intrude on his thoughts. She would call Jeremy Brenner and Allistair after a quick breakfast.

David's night had been much more complicated than Ma's. At the moment she was contemplating breakfast, he was standing at the long windows of his apartment, misting his precious orchid collection.

Sosam had driven them to the Colony for dinner and the live entertainment they featured in their Polo Restaurant. Not the easiest place for David to eat, but he had planned to work it out.

At the valet station they met up with Jet Carlson and her wife Christy, as well as Barry and his husband Don. Jet and Christy had just arrived and were handing their car key to the bored looking, but polite valet. Summer season was in.

"We were just leaving," Don said. "Frank, Stuart, and Mike are at HMF. It is *the,* hot place to go these days. Interested in joining us?"

Christy immediately swiped their car key from the valet. "I am *dying* to go there," she said looking at Jet excitedly. "We are in," she told Don.

Sosam was practically bouncing up and down. "Yes!" he said. "I have heard it is *fabulous*!" He stopped and looked at David. "Do you mind? It is also very pricey."

David laughed softly. "Money is the last thing I am concerned about in being out with you tonight Sosam." The other man smiled, looking slightly embarrassed. "Please join us ladies," David said to Jet and Christy. "My treat. So leaves tomorrow for school in California."

"Done!" Christy said, pulling Jet back towards their car.

Barry was looking pointedly at David and then Sosam. "Meet you there?" he said, his tone of voice betraying his curiosity.

"Sounds good," David replied, giving nothing away with his neutral expression. Barry watched as David followed Li back to his car.

"What is that all about?" Barry asked Don after they retrieved their own car and headed for the Breakers.

"I am sure I don't know," Don answered grinning.

HMF, a glamorous rewind of Palm Beach's golden era at the Breakers was the *it* place to go. The moniker stood for Henry Morrison Flagler, the Breakers' founding father. Designed by Adam D. Tihany, it was set on the site of the historic Florentine Room.

Sosam was amazed at the elegant ambiance. David smiled as he watched the tall, younger, Asian man hold out his hands and pivot around, taking it all in. Hard muscle from years of martial arts wrapped a slender frame. A modern cut styled his straight black hair around a handsome face.

"I'm glad you are happy So," David said to him. He had called Li by that shortened nickname for years. "Please enjoy every minute and have whatever you want."

Li looked at him and smiled. "You know what I want."

Jet and Christy were also admiring the place and chattering away with Barry and Don. Frank, Stuart and Mike greeted them and they all sat at a casual grouping of club chairs and tables. Delicious small plates and inventive cocktails came and went in waves.

David noticed two men watching the group from one area of the bar. They didn't fit the glittery, Palm Beach scene. They looked more like thugs hired to protect the glittery, Palm Beach scene. Thugs that didn't drink at the bar.

Tiger senses tingling, he decided to find out if he was the target of their interest when Don said loudly, "So David, you and Dr. Ma are helping the police with another murder case here on the island?"

One of the thugs nearly spilled his drink, his head whipped around so fast at that comment. "So, they are listening to our group," David thought. Aloud he said, "Yes, we just got back from Manhattan." The thug leaned so far towards him, the stool he was sitting on was in danger of tipping over.

"So cool," Mike and Stuart said in unison. "Do tell!"

"I really can't share anything of course," David said. Stuart pouted disappointedly. "If you all will excuse me, I am going to find the men's room." Very quietly, under his breath, David leaned close to Sosam and said, "Stay here please. Don't let anyone follow me."

Li nodded without looking at him. David was still his teacher. He knew about taking direction from him. "Don't be long," he said to David, smiling. Jet had caught the subtle interaction and was looking at him with narrowed eyes. Everyone else at the table was oblivious, enjoying their cocktails and bites of elegantly plated food.

Walking directly up to the bar the thug was leaning against, David smiled at the bartender and asked where the men's room was. The man politely pointed it out, all the while polishing and stacking glasses.

David walked away, happy to notice one of the thugs following him. Just out of sight of his friends, he took a quick turn and exited a glass door onto the beach. The thug followed closely.

Walking far enough onto the beach he took another turn to place them out of direct sight from the hotel staff and guests.

David stopped and turned towards the man following him. The thug frowned and pulled out a semi-automatic pistol. A silencer was fixed onto the end of the barrel. "I have a message for you," the thug said menacingly.

"I hope it's a short one," David said and closed the gap between them in a blur. Reaching across his body with his left hand, he bladed his body to the side and stripped the gun from the man's hand. The weapon flew several feet, landing in the sand. Reversing his bladed position, David's right hand smashed into the thug's face, dropping him instantly.

The man's nose split open like a squashed tomato from the blow, but he wouldn't know what happened for some time. He would know it when he finally woke up.

David looked up just as Jet came running out onto the sand. "Behind you!" she said.

David turned to see the other thug holding a match to the weapon resting in the sand. Too late, he felt the impact of the bullet on his lower back above his right hip. It turned him more fully towards the newly arrived bad guy.

He saw the second thug raise the weapon, pointing towards Jet and lunged at him. David had a human body but it was preternaturally fast. He hit the thug mid body before the weapon finished its upward trajectory. The impact produced a loud 'crack' from the second thug and he landed unconscious, backward in the sand.

Growling softly, in pain and bleeding from his gunshot wound, David grabbed both of the unconscious thugs and dragged them toward the ocean. "Pick up their guns and come with me," he said to Jet.

At the water's edge, he placed both men face down and taking the guns from Jet, threw both far out into the water. "You're going to leave them here to drown?" Jet asked.

"I'm leaving them here," David answered angrily. If they don't regain consciousness before the tide comes in, I guess they will drown. It's up to the Universe to decide their fate."

"You are bleeding, or you were bleeding," Jet observed as they walked back to the patio doors they had originally come through. She lifted his jacket to look at the gunshot wound through the hole in his white shirt. "I know what you are David," she said. "My family," she began.

"Yes, yes, I know about your family David said, grimacing with pain as he sat on a small bench just outside the glass doors. "Sit with me a moment?" he said shyly.

She smiled and sat next to him. Gently she reached over and placed her hands on his back and abdomen. He felt an almost immediate relief of pain. "Thank you," he said. "I will heal quickly, but I am not sure what to do about the shirt."

She looked down and said, "There is only blood on the shirt, not the pants or the jacket really. You seemed to stop bleeding almost immediately."
David buttoned his jacket. "Will that work?"

"Yes," she laughed. "Can't see a thing, but get undressed in the dark when you take Sosam home tonight. Don't want him to freak out."

"Right," David said. Then he looked at her with a slight frown. "How do you know I will be getting undressed around Sosam tonight?"

"Please!" she snorted. "You are going to cave and give him what he wants. For the record, I tried to get him to change his mind. I knew you were too nice to refuse him under the circumstances."

Before he could answer her, David's phone rang. David answered it and Allistair started talking as soon as he accepted the call.

"Do you need cleanup? What happened? Are you okay? Who is the girl?" all came out in a rush.

"Everything is fine. I already cleaned up, sort of, and I seem to be pretty much healed. That is Jet next to me. Don't you recognize her?" David said patiently.

"Jet?" Allistair said, sounding confused for a moment. "Oh yes, her family…"

"Yes, I know about her family," David said. "Look I have to get back inside before someone comes looking for us."

"Call me if you need anything. Those were Cohen's men according to the facial recognition on the security tape. Guess he isn't happy with you and Dr. Ma. Good job."

David shook his head at the speed of Allistair's spy network. It had kept them safe and alive for millennia. These days it was beyond high tech. "Let's get inside," he said to Jet.

Sosam was coming towards them as they walked back into the elegantly appointed room. He looked pointedly at their slightly disheveled appearance and said, "Should I be jealous?"

Jet rolled her eyes and headed towards the ladies room. David stepped closer to his longtime student. "Do I look that bad?" he asked.

"Nothing that a quick touchup in the men's room won't fix," Li answered, looking at him curiously.

I'll explain later So," he said. "Give me a minute while I go to the men's room."

"No," Li answered. "I'm coming with you. This could be the best night of my life and I am not losing track of you again until it's over."

They both laughed and walked toward the men's room. Back at the group, a few minutes later, David noticed Jet looked like nothing had happened on the beach. She smiled and nodded. Barry and Don stood up when they returned. "Time for the old guys to leave," Don said.

"We should get going too," David added. "Sosam has to fly out tomorrow, big day."

"Big night," Christy said, slightly slurring her words. "He is going to take David home and blackmail him into sex."

"She is drunk," Jet said quickly, standing up, dragging her inebriated spouse with her. "Time for us to go too." They quickly left the table.

"Blackmail?" Stuart said raising his eyebrows slightly. "Such a handsome man," he said pointing at Sosam Li, "doesn't need to blackmail anyone for sex. Call me if David disappoints you," he said miming a phone at his ear. "Mike falls asleep early."

They all laughed. The group broke up for the night and David and Sosam found themselves outside David's apartment off Peruvian Avenue ten minutes later. "Coming up?" David said shyly, looking at Li.

"Yes," Li answered. "But, not if it's blackmail. I know you don't feel the same way I do. This has to be completely voluntary."

"You are not forcing me So, I just don't know what I am doing here," David answered honestly. "You are, you were, my student and as friendly as I have ever been with anyone in that capacity. This is foreign territory in more than one way. We can give it a try."

Li nodded in agreement and they walked up the narrow stone staircase together. "By the way," Li said as he followed David. "Did you know you have blood on your shirt and a hole that looks like you got shot?"

David sighed, but didn't look back. "I know. I'll take a quick shower first."

Chapter Thirteen - Everybody Talks

Jeremy Brenner's cellphone rang and for a minute he was disoriented. He reached for the side table but there was a warm sleeping body between him and the phone. Then he remembered.

"Morning," he said as Gracie turned towards him. He reached over her and flipped open the phone to answer the call.

"*That* is your phone?" Gracie said surprised. "Oh god, I really did sleep with an old man."

Brenner ignored her and got out of bed quickly, grabbing his every present note pad. "Brenner," he answered.

"Jeremy?" came Dr. Ma's voice. "Are you coming to class this morning? I want to know the plan for tonight, if you can stay afterwards."

"Yes," Brenner said, shifting his phone to the other ear as Gracie planted a quick kiss on his cheek."

"Coffee?" Gracie called over her shoulder, walking towards his kitchen.

"Is that Gracie?" Dr. Ma asked quickly.

"Ah, yes," Brenner answered hesitantly. He was too much of an old fashioned gentleman to say more.

"Good for you," Ma laughed. "She is terrific."

"Agreed." Jeremy sighed. "Will David be at class? I was really blown away by last night. I wanted to ask him a few questions."

"Not likely," Dr. Ma answered. "He is off." She didn't want to elaborate. She knew from her earlier conversation with Allistair how David's night had gone and who he was with this morning.

"Too bad," Brenner said, sounding disappointed. "Everything is set for tonight. Is he going to be available for that?"

"I'm sure he will be available tonight," Ma reassured the detective. "Jeremy?" she said.

Gracie had returned with two mugs of coffee and was trying to get him back in bed before they had to get ready for class. Her hands had the rough calluses from years of training underneath, but on top. looked like they belonged to the very pretty woman using them all over his body.

"Yes?" he said, trying to avoid getting overly distracted while he was still on the phone.

"It looks like Cohen may have had someone following David last night," she said.

Suddenly all business, Jeremy sat up straight and grabbed both of Gracie's hands. "What?" he said, louder.

"It was at the Breakers. He said they confronted him when he went to the men's room, but something or someone spooked them and they took off," Ma explained.

Jeremy quickly snapped open his laptop on the nightstand. The screen came to life with a new email from the police department. A bulletin noted that two men were found battered on the beach by the Breakers last night, but they refused to cooperate when authorities were called.

"I think I have some information on that," he said slowly to Dr. Ma as he read.

"Great," she said. "We will discuss it later. Say hello to Gracie for me. Don't be late for class." She hung up long before Brenner closed his phone. He was reading over the email again. He typed off a quick response to the shift commander that put out the bulletin.

Gracie had gone back to kissing his neck and back, her hands exploring his body like the new toy that he was. "We have a few minutes," she said, her teeth gently sinking into his ripped abdomen. "Can you handle it old man?"

Putting his phone next to the laptop he smiled and rolled her onto her back in response. His phone rang again after they had finished and he was in the shower. David left a message that he would see him later today and that he had a run in with two thugs working for his suspect, Barry Cohen, last night at HMF.

Grabbing another cup of coffee, Brenner took his briefcase and drove them both to class. He wished he had his issued vehicle. He had left everything else in his unmarked car last night when he drove to class in his POV.

They made it to class in time. Just in time.

David left Jeremy Brenner a message and walked back to his bedroom with a mug of coffee for Sosam and cup of herbal tea for himself. A bowl of fresh fruit and another of nuts accompanied the drinks on the tray. David had already eaten several handfuls of his favorite seed and nut mixture getting their drinks ready.

He stopped in the doorway, not sure if he should wake Li. Last night had been interesting to say the least. He wasn't sure how it was supposed to have gone last night. He had tried. He was even less sure what he was supposed to do this morning. He stood there hesitating.

"Do I get the coffee or are you just going to stand there," Li asked, opening one eye and half sitting up in bed. He stopped to stare at the naked man in front of him, holding the tray. "You are incredibly beautiful," he said.

David put the tray on a low table by the wall. He stood hesitantly at the edge of the low bed frame. He slept on a tatami bed. No matter how much Barry had complained through the years, all David let him change were the tatami squares, not the setup. The bedroom always had to be designed to accommodate that type of bed.

Li reached up and grabbed David around the waist, pulling him down beside him. "So," David said, looking at him seriously. "I am sorry if last night wasn't great for you, I tried."

"Stop talking," Li said, putting his fingers over David's lips. "You were gentle and sweet. It was very genuine. I have been crazy about you since we met. That is exactly what I wanted."

"I really didn't know what to do," David began.

"Again," Li said, kissing him softly. "It was perfect. I don't regret my decision. I think my crazy mind was hoping for a stronger connection but the sex was everything I could have hoped for."

"I can't really *connect* deeply with anyone So," David said, closing his eyes as the younger man trailed his hands along the complex series of tattoos on his abdomen. "I have been in love with just one person forever."

He wasn't exaggerating on the *forever* time frame.

"Sensei, I mean Dr. Ma," Li answered, one hand trailing further down as the design worked its way over David's pelvis and hips.

A soft groan escaped David's lips before answering. "Yes," he said softly.

Li felt a wave of sadness coming from the stunning man laying next to him. "But she does not love you back," he said, more of a statement than a question.

"No, she doesn't," David answered, rolling on his side to face Li. "We have some time before you have to get ready. I would like to take you shopping before you get on the road. Dr. Ma and I were thinking perhaps, a watch to commemorate your new college life?"

"Send me the watch if you like," Li said, wrapping his arms around David and turning the taller man away from him. Li's fingers traced the fine scars along David's back and buttocks gently. "How did you get these?"

"My father," David answered honestly. Li stiffened. "Bastard," he thought. He pressed a soft kiss to the closest one.

"Is that a new tattoo?" Li said, lifting David's right arm and sliding his fingers along the inner bicep.

"Yes," David said, surprised. He had forgotten that the black dragon image had appeared the morning after his beach encounter with Dr. Ma.

Just like the ones on his midsection appeared every re-manifestation on his 16th birthday. The year he died. A thousand years ago. He wondered if any other body markings would appear if he and Ma ever interacted again.

"What do you want to do with your time before you leave?" David asked. Somehow he felt he knew the answer.

Sosam pulled him over to face him again, a grin on his face. "Improve your skills before I go."

At the dojo, students turned, pushed and blocked in graceful harmony. The Tai Chi class was physically demanding, but somehow, it left everyone calm and happy when it was over.

When the form finished, Jeremey thought, "That went well, but there was something different about working with Gracie." The tension between them before had given their practice an edge. Now that they had slept together things seemed smoother.

He noticed Dr. Ma watching them carefully, but she hadn't changed their pairing. "That means it is flowing well," Brenner thought.

After class, Dr. Ma walked him to the back door to pass through the Zen garden. Gracie looked up from her duties with the other students. They all cleaned the dojo after practice. She smiled briefly but gave no other sign that they had a deeper connection now.

Brenner sighed in relief. "This could work," he thought. To Dr. Ma, he said, "I have some information on the two hired hands that followed David last night."

"Great!" she said as they said down in the empty reception area. "Did you get the statement from New York?" She was referring to Pazuzu's social secretary, Scott.

"He was very cooperative, thank you," Brenner nodded. He reached for the box of pastries she had placed on the reception area table before beginning class. A carafe of coffee was next to the box. "It seems too quiet in here without Winnie," he said.

Dr. Ma looked at him for a moment before saying, "Winnie gave her notice Jeremy. She is leaving by the end of the month."

He stared at her for a full second before swallowing a big bite of pastry. Putting down his coffee, and the sugary breakfast he was consuming, he wiped his mouth. "Seriously?" he said.

"Completely," she said. Tears formed at the corners of her eyes. "I will miss her so much."

He moved next to her on the couch and put his arm around her shoulders, not thinking of the possible appropriateness of his response to her tears. She looked up at him in surprise and then laid her head on his shoulder and let the tears flow.

"It's been a tough week," she said. "Thank you."

The detective knew it must have been a helluva week for his friend to be so overwhelmed. She was the strongest person he had ever met. "Pastry?" he said leaning forward and offering her the box. They laughed together, breaking the tense mood. "Are you looking for a replacement?"

"I am leaving it up to her," Dr. Ma said. "She knows the job better than anyone." She said up straighter and grabbed a tissue from the box on the table. "Enough self pity," she said. "Let's talk about the case. Did Allistair give you Kellar's letter?"

"The one his girlfriend took to the police when she couldn't find him at his apartment? Yes," Jeremy replied returning to his chair and snagging another pastry before he put the box down. "Authentic.It matches samples of his writing from the apartment. NYPD forensics agrees. It was smart insurance to detail his involvement to his attorney in case of a *sudden* demise."

"No body was found yet though?" Dr. Ma asked, fully aware there was no body to find.

"No, but the substantive evidence of the statement will be applicable in trial according to the State's Attorney I spoke with," Brenner said excitedly. "Kellar's girlfriend gave it to the NYPD and apparently Allistair had some items of evidentiary value that Kellar had left in a bank deposit box."

"Did you find the missing horn?" Ma asked.

"Yes," he said. "It was wrapped up with a biohazard sticker on it, believe it or not. Then there was a recording of the conversation Barry Cohen had at Kellar's when he gave him the money. The cash was in the box with Cohen's fingerprints. It was great."

"So tonight you are hoping to elicit a confession of some sort?" she prompted.

"Between Cohen and Allistair, yes," Brenner said. "Scott was too scared to get involved, but your attorney is cool as a cucumber. He is just meeting with Cohen to get the sum of his client's payment for the murder. As per Kellar's instructions."

"Please don't think Allistair is involved in this situation and arrest him," Dr. Ma laughed.

"Of course not," Brenner assured her. "He is just acting the part for us. There are no instructions from Kellar to that effect and we have no idea if there was any further payment promised."

Dr. Ma grinned. "This should be interesting. I will tell David what we discussed. I am sure he will enjoy helping out."

"You two are going to be the girlfriend and Scott if needed. Cohen doesn't know what either of you look like. Bridgette did all the interacting with your Manhattan contact."

"Great!" Dr. Ma said. "Have you had enough to eat for breakfast?" She indicated the now empty pastry box and smiled.

Brenner looked guilty for a moment. "You didn't want one did you?" he said.

"No Jeremy," she laughed. "They were all for you. I had breakfast at home this morning. I have a feeling you didn't."

His face turning bright scarlet for a moment, Brenner nonetheless gave her an ear to ear grin. "Nope."

"Good for you Jeremy," Ma said. "She is a lovely young lady. Make sure you both give each other the same respect and time that you do your job and her studies."

"Good advice," he said. "Did it work for you?" He was using his investigative wording to get information from the reticent woman.

She laughed at his effort. "Yes Jeremy, I was in love once in my life. Just once. It worked."

"What happened?" he asked, going for broke. All she could do was refuse to tell him.

She paused, looking at him carefully. "He died," she said. "I have never fallen in love again."

"That is a shame," Brenner said honestly. "You are an incredible woman. I'm sure you have lots of men interested in you." He stopped, remembering holding her on the bench in West Palm during her 'vision'.

"Yes," she said smiling. "Even *you* are nice enough to be briefly interested in an old lady."

His face felt hot again for a moment. It was as if she could read your mind! "I'm sorry if I was inappropriate Sensei," he said.

She laughed again, this time longer. "Not at all! I was flattered by your attraction. I should be less involved in my work and more open to social interactions I guess."

"David is in love with you," he said, knowing he had left the boundaries they had set up between them by a mile. "But you don't love him."

"Oh, I love him," she said, her eyes focused beyond him on something only she could see. "Just not like that. It's a struggle lately." Suddenly she looked at him and stood up. "Ok, enough of the interview detective. What time and where should we meet you tonight?"

Brenner smiled, she was something else. "Royal Palm Way at 7:00 PM. Go shop around the Palm Beach Bookstore there. Candice Cohen is the owner, no relation to the bad guy. She is going to stay open late for you as a favor."

"Allistair is meeting Barry Cohen at Testa's?" she said.

"Yes," he replied, all business now. "Then they will take a walk north towards the ocean and talk so nobody can overhear their conversation. Except us of course."

"You and a dozen undercover officers?" she smiled.

"Exactly," he confirmed. You and David will walk that way when I text you as they leave. Keep an eye out for Cohen's personal bodyguards. They will follow him casually. Stay behind them. We are already set up in the area."

"Sounds great," she agreed. "We will see you there."

David responded to her text as he was heading out for his run.He would meet her at the bookstore at 7:00 PM. It was near enough to his apartment that he could walk. He didn't want her to pick him up anyway.

Sosam Li had left half hour ago. David changed into his HOKA running shoes and a light pair of shorts. He put on the Salomon hydration vest Sam had left for him. Hydration wasn't the only issue for him in getting ready for his ultra distance run with Sam.

The vest held an array of snacks as well as some general essentials. The issue he would have to deal with was his high metabolism. He always needed to eat.

Sam had recommended the vest with a water bladder and pockets for supplies. This would be the first time he tried using it.

When David had carried Karen fifty miles at top speed from their South Africa camp to the Reserve lodge, he wasn't as much thirsty as he was starving when he arrived. Frowning, he shoved another nut bar into the vest pockets.

Running lightly down the steep and narrow stone stairs from his apartment to Peruvian, he stopped short as Karen McCarthy walked up to him.

"Hello David," she said with a smile. He felt the odd sensation of cold water being poured into his gut. "Why?" he thought nervously looking around. "I never felt that way around her before."

Aloud he said, "Hello Karen," and tried to step around her on the narrow sidewalk. He just wanted to get going on his run. She put a hand out and wrapped long, slim fingers around his wrist. It felt like electricity running through him.

"Oh bad," he thought. "This is definitely new." He stopped moving, his body shaking from her touch and wondering if he could extract his wrist without looking like a crazy man, yanking away and running like hell.

"Can we talk for a moment?" she said. "I want to apologize for my behavior at the party. How about dinner tonight?"

He looked at her, trying not to betray his anxiety. His whole body was trembling now. He pulled, trying to free his wrist. She didn't let go. "Please. Let. Go," he said in measured beats. "I accept your apology but I am not free for dinner tonight, or any night really. I think we should avoid each other."

Karen's eyes clouded over with anger. The pulse of electricity increased so much, David almost dropped to his knees in front of her. "F-ck it," he thought and rolled his wrist out of her hand in a practiced movement. He stepped back quickly to avoid her reattaching herself.

Lips pressed together with anger, Karen pivoted on her heel and got into her Porsche convertible parked next to the sidewalk. "Watch your back David," she said as she stomped on the accelerator and pulled away from the curb.

Too late, a young woman on a bicycle tried to swerve out of her path. David leapt across the space between the curb and the cyclist and caught the young woman as she was about to crash into another parked car.

"Umph," the familiar looking woman said as he grabbed her and the bike to stop her from crashing. His momentum kept him going and he landed under her. The woman and the bike landed tangled on top of him.

"Crap," David groaned as he gently extricated himself and helped her up. He was cut and bleeding here and there from the road and her bike. "Dr. Ma and I have to do something about Karen before she kills someone. Mainly me," he thought.

"You again!" the woman cyclist said as she untangled herself and checked for damage. She removed her helmet and David recognized the pretty young medic who had been at his two most recent injury calls in Palm Beach. "Peggy James," she said pointing to herself.

"Yes, I remember," David said, walking over to the outside hose beside Renato's. He quickly rinsed off, trying to obscure the fact that his injuries were already healing.

"Thank you!" she said. "That crazy woman almost killed me. I didn't even notice she was pulling out."

"It was my turn to save you," David said, smiling slightly. "Look, I was just going out for my run, are you okay?"

"Fine," she said, looking him up and down. "You hardly have a scratch. Amazing. I was just cutting through to the beach. Maybe I should ride along with you for a bit. I am not on duty today and apparently you are always in danger, even when you are saving someone else from a near death experience."

Chapter Fourteen - How To Kill Your Wife

Dr. Ma and David met Jeremy Brenner at the Palm Beach Bookstore promptly at 7:00 PM. He was chatting with the owner, Candace Cohen, and pretending to be interested in books on their local author rack in the back.

David had seen Allistair sitting with Barry Cohen in the outside table area at Testa's restaurant. Dr. Ma was just getting out of her car after parking in one of the median slots on Royal Palm. He had walked towards her quickly to avoid being recognized by the two thugs from the other night. Both were sitting at another table near their boss, watching Allistair carefully.

Two more similar looking thugs had been standing by a black Town car, parked in a parallel spot near the restaurant itself. "The two in the restaurant are the ones from the other night," David told Brenner.

"At HMF?" Brenner clarified. "The ones found semi conscious on the beach? Beaten up? Not willing to tell us what happened?"

"Okay," David said to him. "I am sensing sarcasm in your tone Jeremy."

Brenner smiled. "Not at all. I believe you when you say they just warned you to stay away from the murder case and walked away. Someone else must have had an issue with them."

"Even I am hearing sarcasm," Dr. Ma interjected. The store owner had walked into the back during this part of their conversation, so they were speaking more openly.

"We will stay well out of sight when we follow them," Dr. Ma said.

"Sounds good," Brenner said. He looked at his phone. "They are moving, let's go." He called a brief good bye to the owner and they walked out into the velvety South Florida evening.

Allistair handed Barry Cohen a sheaf of papers. "This should give your accountant the information he needs to transfer the balance of Mr. Kellar's money to his account. Everything is held in trust for his nephew.

"You are f-cking crazy if you think I am leaving any kind of paper trail," Cohen said in his raspy voice. He sounded like an aging gangster from days gone by. "I don't owe that bastard anything. He did a f-cking lousy job."

"Your wife is dead." Allistair observed dryly. He was dressed, as usual, in an immaculate and perfectly tailored three piece suit and tie. "Sounds like the contractual obligation was fulfilled."

Cohen stopped and pointed his finger at Allistair. "Look McGowan, she was supposed to be left in that apartment in Manhattan. I really hate that guy, what's his name, the satanist guy."

"Pazuzu," the attorney supplied. He looked at Cohen's stabbing finger and smiled. The effect could be chilling. His Snake persona came through his human features easily. "Nevertheless," he continued as Cohen withdrew his finger. "The balance is to be delivered, so cash is fine. I will deposit it."

"You are a ballsy guy," Cohen said, trying to re-establish control of the conversation. "What makes you think you won't disappear like Kellar, eh?"

Allistair smiled again, this time giving the other man a peek at a row of glittering white teeth.

Cohen took a step back. The two thugs following them stepped forward. Cohen held up a hand to stop them.

"I know a great deal about how Kellar disappeared," Allistair said, a slight hissing quality to his voice. "So why did you have your wife killed?"

"She was a freak," Cohen grumbled. "I didn't know that when I married her. Good sex. You know." He looked at the attorney.

"Don't I ever," the other man replied. They had reached the access road that eventually opened up to the east side of the island and the beach.

"I could use a man like you," Cohen said. "It would be better than having to kill you to keep you quiet."

Allistair laughed. "I will take that under consideration. But be assured, you present no threat to me my dear man. Rather, I do, to you."

The shouts of 'Police! Hands up! suddenly exploded in the air. Undercover officers moved in, weapons pointed at five of the men. Allistair laughed again as Cohen looked at him confused.

"Son of a bitch," Cohen said to him.

"Wrong species," Allistair corrected him. He looked past the encroaching officers and saw David and Dr. Ma waiting on the southwest side of Royal Palm and County Road. Smiling, he walked away to join them.

Jeremy Brenner met him and slipped his hand into the fussy attorney's inside suit pocket to retrieve his recording device. He also detached the lapel pin that was a combined video and audio receiver.

"Handsome young men reaching into my jacket, nasty men threatening me and two old friends waiting to take me to dinner," Allistair observed. "Doesn't get better than that! Join us detective?" he said winking at Jeremy.

"Ah, no thank you Mr. McGowan," Brenner answered. "Lots of work left to do tonight. Please stop by the station when you are finished and sign your statement. I'll need it in the morning for his arraignment."

"Will do," the attorney answered.

"Mr. McGown?" Jeremy paused, looking at the older man intently.

"Yes, my boy?" Allistair rumbled.

"Pretty good acting for an attorney," Jeremy said.

"Hmmm," the man answered, and walked off with Dr. Ma and David towards their cars. Dinner had been ordered and was waiting for them at Renato's.

Jeremy Brenner went to the morgue before he finished for the night. He had done everything he could to present an iron clad case against Barry Cohen for killing his wife Bridgette. The rest was up to the State's Attorney.

The detective had a habit of visiting the grave of the victim when things were over to talk to them about the outcome. Bridgette was being cremated and her remains flown home to her father in Denmark.

He stood next to her stainless steel table, pulled out from the bank of chilled vaults that housed the dead. He put a single rose on the drape that covered her body.

"Well, we got him," he said in explanation. "I am sorry I don't know everything that happened to you. I have a feeling someone else had a part in your death my dear, but I haven't found them."

The stillness only deepened when he stopped talking. He shivered a little in the cold and quiet. He really hated coming in here unless it was absolutely necessary.

"As long as your husband goes down for this, it will balance things out. He put everything in motion. I am sorry things ended for you so early on. You missed out on a lot."

The M.E. stuck her head in the room. "Almost done?" she said sleepily. She was pulling an all nighter from another jurisdiction's case.

"Yep," he said, pushing Bridgette's tray back into it's vault. "Thanks."

"Anytime," she yawned and walked away. "You're a weird guy Brenner."

Bridgette had been nineteen when she met Barry Cohen. She was an aspiring model and had been thrilled to have caught the attention of such a wealthy and powerful man.

She certainly wasn't going to get that far on her looks in the brutally competitive world of fashion modeling. Marrying a rich guy who dotes on you was always a good alternative.

She was a fifth wife, young, beautiful, and open to anything that came her way. One of the many reasons Cohen had married her. Until he decided she was too open. Too far left of center.

Bored, young and rich, Bridgette was always looking for the next thing to peak her interest. It certainly wasn't her much older, out of shape, patronizing husband.

Living in Palm Beach was the worst for her. So conservative and laid back in many ways. The apartment in Manhattan had been her idea. The funky vibrancy of the city allowed her to touch the dark underbelly of the city from a safe distance.

When she heard about Pazuzu's parties she was beyond excited. Who names himself after an ancient demon? Rubbing shoulders with even greater wealth than her husband possessed, as well as the opportunity for serious debauchery, and you had the ideal setup.

Finally getting the number of Pazuzu's social secretary from a gossipy friend of a friend, she made the call. She was invited to the last social event of her life. Her husband wasn't thrilled.

"What the hell do you want with those satanist f-cking party guys?" he had asked her angrily. "You get crazier every day!"

Ignoring him as she had started to do in the first year of their marriage, she made plans anyway. The night of the party she told him she was going alone. "You will just make me and everyone else miserable," she had said. "I want to have a party like that in our apartment."

"Over your dead body," he said. She wasn't aware he was making a statement versus a threat.

When Bridgette started getting into the darker party crowds in Manhattan, Barry had sought the help of Kellar the magician. Word was, he could make lots of things disappear. Even your pain in the ass fifth wife.

For a price of course.

The announcement that she wanted to go to the party alone had been icing on the cake for Cohen. Perfect alibi. She never came home. Weird thing about it. She ended up frozen on a beach house roof top in Florida.

That wasn't exactly what Cohen paid for, but she was dead after all.

Bridgette had been ecstatic when she arrived at Pazuzu's opulent apartment. The furnishings were old and demonic. The host didn't look a day over forty. The guests were creme de la creme of creepy and rich.

The social secretary had been nervous and chatty. He pawned her off as soon as possible on a guest and beat a hasty retreat. A magician of sorts, the charming man got her a drink and took her for a tour of the apartment before escorting her to the rooftop garden where the real action was taking place.

At some point Bridgette had felt herself fading. Everything around her grew darker and muffled. She felt like the air she took in had no oxygen. Sitting down in a lounge chair was the last thing she remembered as a living being.

Her next thoughts weren't thoughts at all. They were more like experiences. Spiritual experiences.

She saw her body. Yes, she knew she was dead. Some demon like creature with a man's head, ox's body and wings was placing her carefully on a red tiled rooftop of a beach house. In Palm Beach, Florida.

Not far from the mansion she lived in with Barry. Used to live in.

She wanted to scream, to tell someone that she was there. She was dead. The demon creature looked at her as it took flight again. It wore Pazuzu's face. The man who threw the party in Manhattan.

Bridgette looked around frantically for someone, anyone to help her. West of her location was a soft glow. She ran, or rather glided, towards the glow.

When she came over the Okeechobee bridge, she saw a female cyclist heading into downtown West Palm Beach. Slim and fit, a long inky black braid of hair trailed down the woman's back.

Bridgette called to her. She could not hear her own voice, but the cyclist stopped and got off her bike. She looked right at Bridgette. She invited her without saying anything to come to her. To come and tell her what happened.

She went.

After dumping the contents of her memory of death, Bridgette the Spirit felt so much better. So light. The woman quietly told her she could go now. No words were exchanged but Bridgette knew it was okay. The woman would take it from here.

The woman would find her killer and bring him to justice. Turning away from the cyclist and towards a glow that was bigger and brighter than the woman had been, Bridgette the Spirit floated closer and closer. In moments she was gone from the Earthly plane of existence.

She never knew her husband was arrested, her killer was eaten by an ancient Storm Spirit who empowered him, or that the man who hosted the party had killed her accidentally.

She would have died anyway. Eventually. Perhaps being frozen while still unconscious was better that suffering from a lethal dose of poison. Although, when you're already dead, these things cease to be important.

You start planning the next time around. Hopefully you do better.

Chapter Fifteen - Life Goes On

Peggy James had offered to ride with David on Sunday for 80 miles while he ran. It was good training for his upcoming hundred mile run with Sam Lightner.

She said she would carry **all** his supplies but he had declined. He had to carry them himself on the race route. At least ten miles worth. That is where each available refueling station was set up. She carried seven pre packaged and measured out water and food setups for him and something similar but not as strictly designed for herself.

Eighty miles was a long ride, but not by much. She was used to seventy miles on the weekend with her group. That ride would only take half as long as David's run, so she would just suck it up.

There was no real down side riding along with the stunningly handsome man who ran faster than any human being she had ever seen. Even some of the cyclists who passed them were surprised at her pacing him so quickly.

She mostly rode behind him, enjoying the view of long, powerful legs ending in a muscular backside tucked into snug shorts. He wore a hydration vest with his water and supplies over a thin t-shirt to avoid chafing.

Still, the view was pretty amazing. She was pinching herself that they were almost dating. If that was what you call being saved from a crazy driver, dinner, a long walk, sex, and then a quick cup of coffee this week.

He was ridiculously sweet and almost shy. How someone that looked like him was so, well, inept in so many ways was beyond her. He had warned her he was not at all like his reputation.

When he asked her to dinner the day she was almost run over, she asked him what he was looking for. He had looked at her confused, like a an excited puppy who accidentally did something he wasn't supposed to, but didn't know why.

"You have quite the reputation," she told him.

He had flushed, his cheeks a gorgeous dark pink under his golden tan. "I've heard," he said. "I assure you I have no idea where it came from. I am nothing like that version of me."

"Really?" she had teased. "What are you like exactly?"

"A much more pathetic version," he had answered truthfully.

"Do you have random sexual encounters with people from Palm Beach parties?"

"In reality or in their imagination?" he asked.

She had laughed. "I hear you swing both ways and aren't often alone."

"I wouldn't classify my attempts at relationships with either sex smooth enough to swing. I am often alone if you don't count working most of the time. My job and my orchids are my most constant companions."

"I don't believe you," she had said.

"Accept my dinner invitation and see if I am not able to underwhelm you with my smooth moves," he said smiling.

"Hmmm," she replied, looking him up and down. She noticed he blushed slightly. "That is really cute, that blushing thing you do. Either it's genuine, or a great fake out."

"I would stop doing it if I could," he said, looking embarrassed. "Look, I would like to take you to dinner, think about it and text or call me, but no pressure. Especially if you think I am playing you. I will never live up to my false reputation, so I would rather not make a fool of myself trying."

He turned away to start his run, waving and giving her a slightly sad smile.
She took the chance. "Tomorrow? About seven?"
He looked surprised, then smiled shyly.
"Renato's? I am vegan, mostly raw, if that doesn't bother you. They are pretty good to me, making what I can eat."

She had accepted and they had a wonderful time. They talked all through the meal and for two more hours walking along Worth Avenue. They ending up sitting on a bench at the beach.

When she yawned, he had quickly made apologies for keeping her so late and walked her back to her car. Kissing her gently on the cheek, he told her that he ran most mornings early and would treat her to coffee at Starbucks before her shift if she was interested.

"David?" she had asked him as he stepped back to allow her to drive away.

"Yes?" he said. His unique lapis blue eyes almost seemed to glow in the hazy street lamps.

"Are you gay?" she asked.

He stood there for a moment, looking at her as if trying to understand the question. "I am probably bisexual," he said, "but I think I need more experience to make that determination."

She laughed and got out of her car to stand in front of him. She reached up to place her hands behind his neck. Pulling his face towards hers she kissed him. Her body pressed into him and he slipped his long arms around her back and buttocks, pulling her closer. Feeling him respond to her, she pulled away and said, "Definitely bisexual at least."

She could tell he was blushing slightly, even in the hazy light. "Sorry," he said. "I didn't mean to..."

She interrupted him with another kiss and said, "I know where you live, is it too soon to take me home to meet your orchids?"

In response, he had picked her up easily and walked up the narrow stone stairs to his apartment. He was incredibly strong. She wasn't a large woman, but nobody had ever made her feel like she weighed nothing more than a doll.

Spending the night with him had been dreamlike. Gentle, shy and inexhaustible, she knew he hadn't been stretching the truth when he said he was not at all like his reputation.

He introduced her to his orchids. Massive flower heads topped elegant roots, stretching the length of the glass windows in the main room. She was touched by the almost frightening sense of physical power he exuded, paired with his gentility in raising the fragile looking blooms.

His love making had been careful and measured but explosive. For her. He was quiet and calm. When she had gotten too rambunctious, he softly asked her to be patient with him and slow down. She didn't know it was almost a life and death requirement.

David was still an Elemental Tiger. Everything that was emotionally charged had to be approached with caution and control. Transitioning with a human could be life changing. For both of them. He had taken her to breakfast the next morning.

A coffee date had gone well a couple of days later. They seemed comfortable with each other in a very short period of time. That is when he told her about his upcoming hundred mile run. Interested in the process as well as him, made her offer to pace him and dump her regular group.

Now she rode along, watching this incredible athlete ticking off the miles in front of her and wondering how she had gotten so lucky.

In his West Palm Beach apartment, Jeremy Brenner was feeling pretty lucky himself. Gracie and he had spent every night together since the first one. She had moved enough of her personal things to his place to make coming and going easy.

He kept thinking that such a young and ambitious woman was not going to stay with him forever. She would realize her Olympic sports dream and leave him behind to do his job in Palm Beach.

Work had been slow but steady after the last case was solved. He had never expected to have homicide cases at all in Palm Beach. He wasn't even sure that his chief was glad he had hired him.

He spent more time at the Mugen dojo than he ever had. Dr. Ma was teaching most of the classes now that Sosam Li had departed and David was gearing up for his big race with Samuel Lightner.

Gracie and Jeremy offered to add themselves to Sam's regular race crew to make up for David's presence. Dr. Ma would have to stay behind and run the Clinic and martial arts school.

Not that she nor David seemed to mind. Brenner was uneasy at the cool distance that seemed to have developed between them lately. David had started dating a Palm Beach Fire Rescue medic.

Pretty thing. Jeremy had interacted with her at many scenes. She was a nice girl and David seemed happier than he had seen him in awhile.

Dr. Ma seemed to busy herself with work and Winnie's upcoming departure. "The announcement that Winnie was leaving hit David hard," Brenner thought. He was there having lunch with them when she broke the news to 'her boys' as she called them.

Jeremy didn't bother to tell her that Dr. Ma clued him in from the beginning.
He thought David looked like he was going to throw up. But he had kept it together.

When he told Gracie, she had asked what the job entailed. Working for Dr. Ma and David would have been a perfect fit for her. More exposure to the two martial arts masters and free classes.

Dr. Ma told him to have her put an application in with Winnie. Even the salary would be better than her part time job at Palm Beach State College's student library.

Winnie was so pleased with the serious and efficient young woman, that she was already trying her out for two weeks. Dr. Ma had assured Jeremy that unless Gracie had some hidden flaws nobody knew about, the job was hers.

Gracie and Dr. Ma seemed to get along very well. On time, professional, caring towards the patients and no nonsense were Ma's basic criteria. Gracie seemed to have everything needed to learn to run the clinic.

David and Gracie were a different version of David and Winnie. The older woman was teaching the younger one how to mother, bully and protect her slightly scattered new charge.

Despite the smooth transition, nobody talked about how much Winnie would be missed. She was a fixture in Dr. Ma and David's lives and that didn't change. Even with a near perfect replacement.

The two Elementals were cautiously working around their relationship in the Clinic and the martial arts school. Ma invited David to dinner one morning during a run.

"Thank you for running with me so early Ma-sama," he said to her. They were getting on the road at two o'clock in the morning to allow his human body to adapt to the stress of long distance running without breaking down.

They were speeding along the trails and paths of a local park area, their predator vision making the effort easy without the need for headlamps.

"Best not to showcase your speed on public roadways," Ma grinned. "Peggy seems to enjoy riding with you as much as Sam does running with you, but I know you are struggling a bit."

"It is hard to moderate the pace to their expectations," David agreed somewhat sheepishly. "Sam is already looking at me like I am some sort of freak of nature.

"You are a freak of nature," Ma laughed. "You seem stronger since the beach. I see you have my tattoo."

David stopped, looking at her uncomfortably and raising his arm overhead to show her the delicate outline of a dragon in his inside bicep. "I didn't expect this," he said. "Is it similar to how the others show up on my sixteenth birthday?"

"Similar," she agreed. "A different source. Look David, I want to discuss something with you I found out recently. Can you come for dinner tonight?"

They had started running again. The dark trees and brush were a blur on either side.

"Sure," he agreed. "Is everything ok? We haven't had a good sit down in awhile."

"I know, and I am sorry," she said, increasing her pace to get in front of him on a narrow section of single track. "We will tonight."

Their clinic day went smoothly with the addition of Gracie in training with Winnie. Seven new patients for David. He was getting busier and busier with his internal medicine practice. A unique fitness and nutrition approach with plant based diet was bringing him as many new faces as his schedule could allow.

Dr. Ma was elbow deep in Summer Triathlon and Endurance athletes. A new ultra runner with a knee and foot injury greeted David as he came into the reception area. "I heard you are giving Sam Lightner a run for his money this year," the man said.

The Swedish born ultra runner had recently moved to the area and was training for his fourth Badwater race.

"Sam was a top 10 finisher last year," David answered. "He talked me into Burning River the year before and I put my name in for the lottery. Unfortunately, I got in."

The other man laughed. "Now you have the right attitude. Do you expect to keep pace with Sam?"

"I was thinking about beating him this year so I can shut him up," David responded seriously.

The other man laughed, then stopped. David appeared serious. He figured he was either kidding or things were going to be interesting this year. Taking a closer look at the tall man in the lab coat, dress shirt and pants, he tipped his head slightly. It was hard to tell, but he had that lean and intense look. "Go for it," he smiled.

"Will do," David replied. "Winnie, I mean Gracie," he said to the younger and older women behind the desk. "All set for the day? Dr. Ma is expecting me for dinner and I wanted to run home if I'm finished."

"You are all set Dr. Anderson," Gracie replied efficiently. "Jet has the evening class and Dr.

Ma is almost done herself. I will tell her you left."

David smiled at the new patient as he left. "Good meeting you Lucas," he said.

"You too," the man replied. He went out the front door of the clinic and sat in his car a moment answering some texts on his phone. Shortly after, he saw David emerge from behind the building in just a pair of snug running shorts and sneakers.

"Well, that answers that question," he said to himself. Out of his business attire, the young physician looked every bit the high level endurance athlete. "I can't wait to see the lineup this year," the man said softly to himself before driving off.

After dinner, Dr. Ma and David walked out to the warded swinging bench in her back garden. She still hadn't told David the key to getting into the area without her. "Try to sit down on the bench all by yourself," she urged.

David looked at her hesitantly. They had talked more than they had eaten for the past two hours. She brought him up to date on everything she had learned and her trip to see the creator. They seemed to be in sync with everything again.

The only thing she wouldn't let up on was making him stronger. He was more than ambivalent on her methods. "Ok," he said, but how painful will it be if I can't?"

"Put your hand out and test the ward," she said. "That way it's just a small shock instead of a big jolt."

"Comforting," he said and put out his hand. No shock came, but the air seemed to trap him, preventing his hand from going further. He pulled back and found his hand trapped. He couldn't get in and now, he couldn't get loose. He pulled harder. Now came the shock. "Ouch," he said.

Ma walked up to him, a look of concentration on her face. "Well, we can try again, or you can stay there all night until it lets you go."

"No, serious?" he said. "I don't want to try again. You know my feelings on this."

"I do," she said looking at him, her face softening. "You just don't have a choice in this matter. I told you what the creator and Kaia said."

David gave another yank on his hand. This time the jolt of pain dropped him to one knee but didn't release him. "No," he said softly. "They didn't say it had to be the way you are offering to do it."

"No, they didn't say my way was the only one," she agreed. "I choose not to take you as a mate. It is wrong for me. Sharing my energy with you I can do. I'm sorry David. I know that is not what you want."

He stood up and looked at her, saying nothing. She walked closer and put her arms around him, transitioning seamlessly into her Dragon form. "Bring me the Tiger," she said in his mind.

He tried. Something just wouldn't let him transition for her. He trembled at the effort. She bared her sharp teeth and wrapped her long and powerful wings around him to hold him up.

In his human form, her powerful Elemental energy washing over him was almost intolerable. She opened her mouth to bite him as she had done before. Her talon like finger nails dug into his buttocks through the soft faded jeans he wore.

"No, don't," he protested weakly. Despite the waves of sexual response overwhelming him, he would have opted out. If he could. If any part of him was still under voluntary control. She bit into his shoulder lightly.

The same electrical shock of a thousand knife points hit him and his body tensed, back arching. It seemed stronger this time. His mouth opened, but no sound came out. Her long Dragon's tongue slid roughly over his bleeding wounds, healing them instantly.

When she let him go this time, he slid to ground as before, shaking, unable to stand on his own. She knelt beside him. "I have to visit Paz in New York tonight," she said. "It looks like you are able to get into the ward."

He could see that he was leaning against the bench. He still couldn't speak. He felt tears of frustration and anger slide down his cheeks. "Why?" he tried sending to her mentally. Even gathering his thoughts was difficult.

"Because I love you my Tiger," she said. Standing, she turned away and ran towards the retaining wall onto the Intracoastal waterway. Leaping over it, she took flight soundlessly into the night.

David let himself lie on the ground, no longer trying to stand or control his trembling body. He stayed there for some time, crying softly in the night.

Allistair, Tam and Berenice watched the scene unwillingly from behind the veil of energy that Mort rushed up and threw in front of them before David could notice they were there. The veil obscured them from him, but not him from them.

Berenice turned silently towards the other two. Allistair had brought Tam there to take him into the library. The attorney was trying to research an important connection between Karen and her ability to manipulate objects as Wind Spirits do.

A tear traced it's way down Berenice's cheek. Her eyes were the vibrant lapis blue of all Otherworldly beings.

Allistair knew she felt deeply for David's suffering. Even Tam shuffled uncomfortably next him. The Wind Child was looking down, periodically clearing his throat.

"Ready Berenice?" Allistair said. The beautiful woman nodded and the three of them disappeared from the Earthly plane, leaving David alone in the dark.

Epilogue

Buddha always said that attachment is what causes mankind pain.

Pain from unrequited love. Pain from the loss of life of a family member or loved one. Pain from unfulfilled desires.

It is true, as he said, that we should strive for compassionate detachment. We are ultimately responsible for only ourselves.

Kaia watched David curled up on the ground by the warded arbor. "I warned you," she whispered softly. "I warned you that you would suffer. You accepted the Creator's offer freely."

The ancient tree guardian's voice came to her lightly, on a breath of air. She wasn't fully manifested on the Earthly plane. Her Spirit moved fluidly north from David's location and became tangible just off the walking path along Flagler Drive. Standing next to Jamil's tree, nobody but the nearby Otherworldly beings could see or sense her presence.

"He had no idea what that offer would entail," Jamil's low and gravelly voice chided her.

"I know," she responded and sighed.

"Great Mother," a metallic voice chirped next to the two ancient entities. The Water Sprite stood on the low concrete wall that divided the Intracoastal Waterway from the walking path along Flagler Drive.

"Yes child?" Kaia smiled at the tiny creature.

"It has entered the Earthly realm," the Sprite said with its head bowed in respect.

Kaia touched Jamil's tree briefly. "I have to go old man. Make sure Dr. Ma knows about this," she said.

"Most assuredly," Jamil rumbled.

Kaia shimmered briefly and disappeared. A soft splash announced the departure of the Sprite.

Jamil stepped easily from his tree residence. The powerful Spirit stretched, like someone waking from a long sleep. Fixing an image of Dr. Ma in his thoughts, he too shimmered and disappeared.

The soft, velvety South Florida evening became still again. For now.

About the Author

Lenore Maio is a Florida Licensed Acupuncture Physician residing in Palm Beach County Florida, the setting for the Dr. Ma Mystery series books.

Dr. Maio worked in emergency field medicine and law enforcement before attending graduate school and opening her Traditional Chinese Medical practice.Her speciality is sports medicine.

Dr. Maio is a long distance runner and cyclist as well as an avid gardener.

See more about the author, and other books she has written, at www.drmamysteries.com.

Coming soon…

"Pinprick"
Book Four in the Dr. Ma Mystery Series

Preview

Introduction

When does a small event transcend through time, growing ever larger, until it breaks free into a full blown act of chaos?

Why, every day of course.

This is the cycle of things as we know them. Birth, growth, life and death. Plans are like this. Thoughts morph into ideas and ideas into plans. Plans become actions and actions produce chaos.

The whole thing implodes or explodes, change occurs and we begin again.

Reacting to the end product is my job, what I sign up for every next time around. My name is Dr. Ma and I am an Elemental Dragon

I reside on the Earthly plane in my human guise, with my ever present companion of over a thousand years, David, and my closest friend, Allistair McGowan.

David is an Elemental Tiger, younger than Allistair and I. He is my second Tiger. My balance of energy. My first mate passed long ago from this Earthly plane.

Allistair is an Elemental Water Snake. An Anaconda to be exact. He is also the solicitor of my and David's wealth and holdings on Earth. One has to have resources to do your job you know.

Like I was saying, David and I are usually putting a cork into an end product to help humans and protect them from the evil acts of certain Otherworldly beings.

Now and then, once in a great while, we get to derail the small event, and prevent it from growing into chaos.

This is one such story.

Chapter One

The big cat stalked them as they ran along the American River Canyon Trail section. A fatal cougar attack had occurred days before the race began, but wildlife officers and race volunteers had been increased to cover any eventuality.

The last fatal cougar attack occurred to a forty year old female long distance runner in this very area over twelve years ago. It couldn't be the same animal the experts had said.

The Western States 100 Mile Endurance Run was tough, presenting all sorts of challenges to the participants. Especially the wildlife. Nobody expected to be safe and pampered. The flurry of activity should keep another attack at bay. Unless the animal were sick. Or rabid.

David knew the big cat was neither sick, nor rabid. He could smell her. She smelled perfectly healthy. She also smelled familiar.

Staying out of sight, the animal stalked them just after they passed the Forest Hill Aid station and headed out to more open territory. "Nothing about this was right," David thought. Sam was running strong, unaware of the cat's presence.

They were over 60 miles into the race.
Suddenly the air was split by the characteristic
scream of the cat. Even with headphones on,
Sam pulled up short, yanking his earbuds out
and looking at David in alarm.

"What the f-ck?" was all he said. A scream rang
out, this one human and nearby. Ahead of them
on the trail, another scream and then silence.
Sam was yanking his cellphone out of his race
vest to call for help. "No reception," he said,
turning to David.

David was gone. Sam whirled around in a
panic, looking for his race companion. "David!"
he shouted.

Ahead of him, David had just reached the site
of the cougar attack. A young woman on
horseback had apparently been the target of
the attack. She lay face up on the hard terrain,
her throat torn open.

The cat was standing next to her. It perked its
ears at David's approach and walked towards
him . Her horse was running away from the
scene at top speed. David transformed before
he stopped running into his massive steel grey
tiger. The fine black stripes shimmered in the
light.

In a split second, he was on the cougar, snapping its neck. The animal didn't seem to fight back or try to run when the Tiger leapt at her. By the time he stepped back from the cougar's body, he was in human form again. Everything happened so fast, it took him a moment to realize what he had done.

"Is this some of what you have given me Ma-sama?" he thought, confused and a little afraid. He heard his name being called and saw Sam running up to him, holding his cell phone.

"Oh my god," Sam said, looking down at the dead woman. "Who shot her?"

"What?" David said, walking over to where Sam stood and looking down. Sure enough, a single gunshot wound was visible in the middle of the woman's forehead.

The torn throat was also visible, but he realized no blood was coming from the wound. "She was already dead," he thought. "So, who had screamed?" Cougars will attack if you play dead. Only she hadn't been playing.

Enjoy your preview? Pre-order it now on Amazon Kindle!

For further updates go to www.drmamysteries.com. Get on the author's mailing list, read her blog, learn about new titles coming out!

Thank you for being a fan!

www.ingramcontent.com/pod-product-compliance
Lightning Source LLC
Chambersburg PA
CBHW061538170626
46811CB00001B/27